A DAY TO REMEMBER TO FORGET

A DAY TO REMEMBER TO FORGET

by

ROSALIND BRACKENBURY

introduced by

MARGARET DRABBLE

and with a prefatory note by the author

ADELAIDE
MICHAEL WALMER
2020

A Day to Remember to Forget first published 1971
© Rosalind Brackenbury 1971

Introduction first published in this edition
© Margaret Drabble 2019

Prefatory note excerpted from *Notes on a Writing Life* blog
© Rosalind Brackenbury 2019

This edition published 2020 by

Michael Walmer
9/2 Dahlmyra Avenue
Hamley Bridge
South Australia 5401

ISBN 978-0-6486909-2-4 paperback

INTRODUCTION

A Day to Remember to Forget is one of those books that stands at a significant moment of social history, looking both ways. It is Rosalind Brackenbury's first novel, published in 1971, when the momentum of change in women's lives was gathering speed, and it looks backwards to the time of post-war domesticity and frustration, and forwards to the hope of liberation, self-confidence and self-determination. The Women's Movement had already produced some landmark publications, including Betty Friedan's *The Feminine Mystique* (1963), Germaine Greer's *The Female Eunuch* (1970) and Kate Millett's *Sexual Politics* (1970). Brackenbury belonged to the generation that had absorbed the messages of Simone de Beauvoir's *The Second Sex* (English edition 1953) and was moving on to explore the future of women in fiction, in social studies, in polemic and activism. It has been called the age of 'second wave feminism', but Brackenbury's novel is more complex than that label might suggest.

It is a tolerant, generous exploration of family relationships, of sexual love and marriage in a time of rapidly changing conventions, and of the sadness of the ageing process. Although most of the action is condensed into the timespan of a day, as the title suggests, it explores the past and the future with a non-judgmental sympathy. At the centre of the novel is the Ridgley family, the middle-aged parents leading a regular domestic suburban life of Sunday roasts and lawn mowers and fawn cardigans, and the two sons trying to make sense of their own lives. The older, Andrew, is married with a wife and baby, and the younger, Philip, still a student, is in love with dramatic russet-haired Lucy, who is as alarmed as he is by the threat of the conformity that they fear will overwhelm them if they commit themselves to a conventional middle class married life. They have defiantly chosen to declare their engagement on the day of this family reunion, which marks Philip's mother's birthday, and the announcement does not go down at all well. The young couple are afraid of being dragged down into a world of demanding babies, large meals, and heavy furniture: Lucy, from a more intellectual Bohemian London background, finds suburbia oppressive, and Philip's outburst to his brother, who has reproached him for spoiling their mother's day, strikes many chords. 'What would you have done if you'd been me? Sat there smiling when they said you could fucking well get married when you'd got your fucking degree and respectable job so that you could keep your wife in the turquoise moquette three-piece suite to which she was accustomed?'

That three-piece suite symbolizes the snug shackles of marriage, and the fabric moquette (defined as 'hard-wearing and suitable for public transport') had long been a subject of mockery, even from those (including me) who didn't really know what it was. Note also the casual bad language, to which Mr Ridgley deeply objects: the word 'fucking' had been absent from any but the most avant-garde literature until this period, and also from most middle-class discourse. In 1960, at the trial of *Lady Chatterley's Lover*, the prosecution indignantly pointed out that the words 'fuck' and 'fucking' appeared no less than 30 times, and in 1965 the drama critic Ken Tynan had shocked the British nation by using the word 'fuck' on television. The times were changing, and in this novel we see them in the process of change.

The portrait of the vacillation and uncertainty of Philip and Lucy, poised on the brink of two fateful decisions (to marry or not to marry, to buy or not to buy an impractical and remote but mysteriously desirable house in the country) is teased out with subtlety. Both are equally afraid of sinking into 'the god-awful stinking bourgeois pettiness' of sanctified home life, but despite themselves are taken by the image of Andrew's baby, lying naked on a rug under the lilac tree, and spouting a jet over his nappy and clothes 'like a cherub in a fountain'. Closely observed babies were relatively new in fiction too.

An extra dimension is added to the Ridgley family drama by the watchful presence of their nearest neighbour, the elderly and widowed Mrs Fletcher, who has long lived a vicarious life through the boy Philip. She now invites him and Lucy into her (poetically evoked) darkening and decaying house for a glass of sherry, and hears their plans for and apprehensions about the future, and discusses with them the question of choice — she insisting that 'everybody has some kind of choice'. The tragedy and drama of her past are revealed in retrospect throughout the novel, and are contrasted with the uneventful life of the Ridgleys next door.

But the most telling portrait in the novel is of Philip's mother, the ironically named Felicity Ridgley, who leads a life of quiet desperation. Her days are governed by routine and punctuated by tidying and polishing, by cooking, by meal times, and by worrying about meal times. The birthday menu of roast meat, three kinds of vegetable, apple pie and cream, and cheese and biscuits, dominates her consciousness and is the apex of her day, her 'harvest festival' of family love. But as she presents her offerings she trembles with fear that they will be rejected, that her husband will pause, with the carving knife in his hand, and ask 'How long did you cook this for?' There is a terrible poignancy in this subservience, and yet she is aware enough to resent her servitude, to resent being treated as a housekeeper and scullery maid.

She thinks of her life as a 'sacrifice', but to what has she sacrificed it, and why? Why has she made a martyr of herself? No wonder that Lucy, watching her, is afraid. The novel gives Felicity an unexpected yet wholly appropriate denouement, an ending very much of its time. Brackenbury's analysis of partly self-imposed domestic entrapment is painfully observant and resonant. Do such women still exist? We may fear they do. Their outward circumstances may have changed, but patriarchal attitudes and conventional postures of female subjection persist.

This was Brackenbury's first novel, the prelude to a long and varied career in fiction, poetry and criticism. Later works move into very different and larger spaces, evoking other landscapes (she is very good on a sense of place) and other historical periods. But this novel has a distinctive ring to it. It has caught and transfixed a period, a moment in time. It is a moment I remember well, a moment my mother would have recognised. I can vouch for the authenticity of this account.

MARGARET DRABBLE

London, October 2019.

PREFATORY NOTE

Fifty years ago – can it be that long? Yes, almost exactly. A rather desperate young woman bicycled across Cambridge in the snow to see her therapist, in the winter of 1968-69. She wanted to be a writer. She was a writer. But she was also a wife and the mother of a very small baby, and she was suffering from post-natal depression. The therapist – good for her! – told her to write. Hand the baby to her father, shut the door and WRITE. So she did. She bicycled back, week after week, with bundles of typescript, and she began to feel better. The therapist nodded sagely, and put it in her drawer. After a couple of months of this, the therapist asked "Would you mind if I showed this to a friend of mine, who's a scout for Viking? I think she might like it…"

That was how this novel got published – via the scout, on to Curtis Brown and into the hands of my first agent, Richard Simon, who sold it to Macmillan in London and then to Houghton Mifflin in the US. It was also how my post-natal depression came to an end. I was not only a mother and a wife, but a novelist with a book coming out. It did wonders for my state of mind.

When I got the phone call, the one we writers all dream about, I was living in a flat in Leicester, in the midlands of England, as my husband had a new job there. Depression lurked again – I had not wanted to leave Cambridge and all my friends, but that was what wives did in 1969. It was a year or so later, and I was looking after my daughter and the small son of a neighbour. It was on a Friday afternoon at about four o'clock when the phone rang and it was Richard, telling me that Macmillan wanted to publish my book and pay me three hundred and fifty pounds for it. There is no moment in life that rivals that first time, I think: when you hear that your book will actually be published. I put both children in the bathtub, called the wine shop and asked rather grandly for two bottles of champagne to be delivered. The health visitor came (a woman sent in those days by the Health Service to see how you were getting on as a mother), and the mother of the small boy came to collect him, and I opened the champagne, poured it for them, and we proceeded to get fairly drunk while the children splashed riotously in the bathroom. My husband came home from work and found us all happy and incoherent.

So as my latest novel appears in the US this summer, the first one sticks its head above the waters of oblivion and will have a new life. I'm celebrating both – and as well, the fifty years in between in which I have lived, seen my children grow up, and become - if not the writer I dreamed of being, the one I imagined I was in those heady early days - the writer I actually am.

ROSALIND BRACKENBURY
July 14, 2019

For Miranda

＃ 1

HE walked beside her, loping with a long stride
springing from the knee; he was older than she, and
taller, and he was a man, though the moustache he
had shaved away yesterday had been his first, though
the long bones of his forearms had the delicacy of
boyhood, the quick turn of the wrist from flicking
stones, the fingers nervous from fiddling in trouser
pockets among string and gum and match boxes; he
wore navy blue, his chin propped like a sailor's upon
a high rolled collar that was rough to the touch, his
trousers swinging wide about his ankles, narrow-
booted, slim; and as he walked he was sometimes

silent and sometimes sang loudly a few words of Bob Dylan's song, 'It Ain't Me, Babe', and then again dropped out of noise into silence, leaving the words in the air. She went along with him taking small steps but briskly, her hands in the pockets of her coat and the collar turned up, her boots clicking, so that beside him she was very small and quick and determined. She walked straight, her chin up and hair flowing back in a loose tangle of red and brown, while he was all over the place, missing a note, missing a step, loping sideways like a distracted adolescent cat halfhearted after leaves, a boy kicking a football, spasmodically.

'D'you think we'll get it?' she said.

'Yeah. There can't be all that many people after a place like that. Well, I s'pose you never know. But I should think we'll be O.K.'

'But is it O.K. about the money? I mean, will your parents —'

'Oh, that'll be all right. Hell, it's mine anyway. I'm entitled to it. They'll be so bloody relieved I'm getting married, they won't complain.'

'We couldn't, I suppose,' she glanced up at him, at his sideways face growing out of the collar, 'we couldn't just get it, and go on living together?'

'Don't you fancy it, then? I want to go all patriarchal and have kids and all that.'

'But still,' she said. 'Marriage. What a word, really.'

'It's what you make it,' he said. 'But you don't have to. I mean, you can change your mind.'

'No,' she said, wondering. 'No, that's O.K. If it's

6

the way you want it, I don't mind. It's just surprising, that's all.' A scene in a film, in a picture, on the other side of glass: herself in an apron, sexy with rolled sleeves, scrubbing a table, one of those white wooden ones, with knots; children with proud round heads nodding on frail necks, flowers upon stalks, growing around her; Philip coming in through a door, blocking the light, coming over proprietorially to kiss the nape of her neck. 'It's just that I'm not used to it,' she said. 'You know, it's just that I don't feel old enough.'

'You're old enough.' His smile was suggestive, deliberately, and warmed her; she smiled at him, and skipped to catch up and take his arm, felt the bone through the cloth, the naked man again inside the clothes. 'Sexy thing,' he called her, and she was reassured. But there was so much reassuring to do. As soon as they were out of bed, it seemed, complications flowered from this simple stem, and their words built solid things between them; but she shut her eyes, concentrating, saying 'This is perfection,' and demanded, insisted, that this should be so. The perfect love, the perfect communication, the perfect moment and orgasm and release. The perfect house.

'We won't ever accept second-best. We won't ever become ordinary.'

'Of course not. Hell, if we're intelligent enough to see all this so clearly now.'

'I'll write it in my diary, and make myself read it every ten years. Every five.'

Love came easily, and tears and swift forgiveness; and he calmed her fears by saying that marriage, like the air, was nothing in itself. It was simply there, it was simply the two of them, in their house.

'Four thousand quid for a reserve price!' The woman next to Lucy murmured to her neighbour, loud enough to be heard. 'They must be off their heads. Who's going to pay four thousand for a place like that?'

'Yeah, but they worked on it, ain't they? And they ain't going to see it go for nothing, now. Anyway, with the price of houses, the price of land, you can get anything you want, these days.'

The room was filling with smoke, the tables ringed with the marks of beer mugs glistened as if they sweated. The mugs no longer banged down on the tables under the weight of men's fists but stood about abandoned, the froth shrinking away to the dregs. Faces were no longer bent to suck up the beer through the breaking whitish head but were dry, drawn, intent and turned to a single common point, pared down by caution and avarice to show their likeness one to another; the faces of outdoor men, fenmen and farmers, red from the winds that came straight from Russia across their low-lying land, lined with the effort of tightening the eyes against sun and blowing rain, white across the forehead where the skin hid under hats and caps as they drove their tractors through the mean fen winter days. Philip among them was tall, pale, vacillating. For tonight, Lucy thought, the concentration of eyes that looked out over vast expanses was turned inward; they were like sculptors in stone who abandon the body blows of hammer and chisel and try for a moment to

8

manipulate the fine point of a pencil. Eyes shrank to pinpoints, hands shook upon cigarettes as they watched the auctioneer. Nothing was happening. And he, a town man with his quick nervous hands and bitten nails, his dark suit, was like a policeman directing traffic that refuses to move. He paced, he shouted and cajoled, he begged them with his practised hands to commit themselves; and nothing happened.

Lucy was afraid to look up now, afraid to breathe hard, in case the ash drop from the end of her cigarette and commit her to action. Somebody was sending up the bidding, the auctioneer was shooting up through the hundreds and into the thousands and soon would arrive at a price which would mean that all, for her and Phil, was over. Somebody was making something happen, and yet there was silence. She felt the smoky breath of the fen farmers heavy around her and every now and then a glance meet another, scornfully, over her head. By turning her head slightly sideways, she could see Phil's knees in their blue trousers and his hands spread upon them, white marks tense between the fingers and a cigarette burning low against a brown stain. She saw a long slug of ash drop unasked from her own cigarette, which she had not tasted, and heard the triumphant voice, 'Five thousand, am I bid five thousand? Five thousand pounds!' Forty pairs of eyes and the auctioneer's must have seen that ash drop. The silence was profound. Rows of feet in best boots stood stolid on the floor, betraying nothing. Nobody spoke.

'Four thousand five hundred pounds!' There was

anger in the auctioneer's voice. Was he to have come all the way over from town for nothing? Lucy breathed and heard it deflate the silence.

'Four thousand pounds.' The man was weary, sarcastic. The boots on the floor shifted and grated. Something shivered the cloth of Phil's trousers and the cigarette butt wagged up between his fingers. He lifted his right hand and took a long, intense drag. Lucy's eyes followed his hand and rested on his face, turned from hers in profile. But the silence, the rigidity was breaking further, there were murmurs and coughs and men crossed their legs and some got up to stretch, blotting out with their great black bulks the yellowed wall of the pub. Lucy looked about her and back to Phil; a child, he thought, waiting to be told. The auctioneer was coming down from his stand, frowning and pale, and crossing the room with his gaze held high ahead of him, to avoid questions, and men watched him go and then dropped their eyes. Beer mugs, lifted and drained of their dregs, slammed down again; the men hustled through the door to the bar, to fill up. Matches, striking, illuminated intense faces as new cigarettes were lit and old pipes puffed back to life. Lucy and he were now the only ones still seated.

'What's it mean?' she asked him at large. 'What's happened?' He scratched the back of his head and said, 'I don't really know. I don't think anything has. I mean, nobody bid, did they?'

'But he kept on going up! Somebody must have been bidding. I thought it was me, scratching my nose. Or my cigarette, the ash. Phil —' But he was gone, sniffing up a scent; she saw him move down the

10

room slim and unconfident among the shoulders and spreading bellies of the older men, their broad-palmed grasping hands, and she was afraid watching him that they would lose. She saw him talk, his hands coming up to wave hesitantly around an oval shape in the air, gently created in a moment; and then moving more quickly, and the man to whom he was speaking nodding and pointing over to the bar. Her eyes followed the pointing hand, Phil's too. There was the auctioneer, and one of his men beside him, leaning on the bar. A glass of pale whisky sliding across in the wetness of the bar-top came into his hand, the farmers pressed him from behind, something ingratiating in the fixed smiles, hands fumbling in pockets and then reaching to seize the pint mugs by their handles and tip them and swallow and gasp, while eyes remained ruminative, staring out over the rim. They were good-looking men, and they surrounded the pallid auctioneer from Hallett's like curly-coated hunting dogs around a whippet. She strained to catch Phil's eye, for he had gone off leaving all their loose change in her purse, off into the contest with only a cheque book and his smile.

'Are you thinking of buying, my dear?' It was a short round woman asking, eyes anxious on Lucy's level, stroked in with fine lines around the strained blue, cheeks reddened from working in the wind that came over the fens; rough hands reached now to tidy the grey hair back to the nape of her neck in a nervous movement, straighten the scarf at the neck of her good blue dress.

'Is it yours?' She was the only other woman there; they were two, their hands hanging down empty and their voices hushed and polite among these crowds of men.

'Yes, it's ours.' The woman was almost whispering, as if in all that space her voice had forgotten how to pitch, and she feared that she might shout or scream. 'But it does seem to be going badly; oh dear, I can't understand it, really.'

Lucy considered for a moment the wisdom of telling her everything, but her own nervousness spilled out, making it impossible for her to withdraw. 'Oh, well, I hope we can buy it. But what happened? I don't understand, nobody said anything, there weren't any bids, were there? We didn't really understand what was going on.'

'It didn't even reach the reserve price.' She drew herself up, proud after a public shaming; here they were, the two of them, she and her husband, in their best clothes, and nobody had even bid. 'Means something to you, you know. I spent the best years of my life on that place. Worked on it for the best part of my life.'

Lucy's hands came up, to cover and protect, and she felt herself hot with the woman's mortification, with the tension, and the fact that she and Phil had understood nothing of what was happening here. 'Oh, but we want it,' she said impetuously. 'We loved it. We thought it was perfect. We're getting married soon, we need a house. Oh, and it's so incredibly romantic, with that one tree and that amazing countryside.' The woman looked puzzled, but Lucy sighed, 'Oh, I do wish we'd known. I do wish we'd known what was happening.'

'But you should have bid, dear.' The woman's eyes

looked already anxiously past Lucy, searching for her husband at the bar, the blue clearer now with a hard little central flicker of concentration where the humiliation had been; her hand already waved to bring him over, to make everything all right.

'Why didn't everybody else? I mean, what were they all here for?'

'Oh, they just came to watch,' she said with bitterness unconcealed. 'We don't get out much in the evening round here, you see.'

'Oh, I see. I didn't understand, neither did Phil. I thought everybody bid at auctions. I was just waiting for it to start.' She was alight now with the possibility that everything could be changed, so that it would work out perfectly for all of them. It was simple, after all; their luck had not broken; everything would be all right. The woman's tall grey-headed husband was coming carefully towards them, balancing a glass of stout between the pint of bitter and the hand which held his pipe. Beside him, also carrying his pint and one for Lucy, came Phil. She smiled her enthusiasm to him and cried, 'Phil! We made a mistake! Those other people weren't here at all, they only came to watch, nobody was bidding, and it doesn't matter that nobody did, because we can still buy it now, can't we?' she appealed to the farmer's wife. The woman smiled and nodded and gestured with a jerk of her hand to her husband that they should all sit down. They sat, the three of them, and Phil stood, frowning into his beer glass with no word for Lucy, and she felt chilled and excluded all at once, and angry with him for being so aloof. He was so conventional, he would let everything slide out of his grip out of sheer concern for etiquette; he would never do anything, never act. She willed him to act, to succeed for them.

Eventually, slowly, without looking up from his glass, he said, 'How much would you think of accepting?'

'How much would you offer?' The man was slightly mocking, edged with steel; probably with his wife there, and her wanting her new house and her furniture, terrified that they might not get enough.

'Well.' Phil swirled the beer in the glass, still stared into the amber depths. Lucy saw the light through the pink transparencies of his ears. 'I might offer three-five.'

She must cry out, protest, But that's not even the reserve price! But no, she checked herself, a little afraid, and glanced at the man's wife, who had hardly time to spare her one in return.

'Nope.' The farmer looked towards the bar, as if in a moment he might turn his back and be with his companions. 'Not a chance. You're a city man, aren't you? Well, I've worked that six acres for thirty-odd years, and I know it's worth a sight more than that. That's all good fen earth, that is, black and good. You can get spuds out of that, or celery. There's money in celery, right?'

Phil, who did not know, nodded as if he weighed the spuds in one hand against the celery in the other; and Lucy nearly laughed aloud, choked as she was with her nervousness and the thought of Phil planting anything. Grass, they had planned, enough to keep a horse and perhaps some goats to keep down the undergrowth; she would pick mushrooms on

14

misty mornings and pull up delicious lettuces to prepare with dressing for Phil's supper. Six acres of potatoes, in black earth; they would never have time off from either planting them or digging them up.

'Four hundred an acre, that's what they reckon round here for good land like that. So that makes it, six acres, two-four without the house. And that's a good house. Worth at least four, that house.' There had been a wide farm kitchen, low-ceilinged, with a big window out to the whole sweep of the fen, away to the curved horizon; a bedroom with the wind in the tree's branches outside; but she had not thought that they would have to pay for all those potatoes.

'Four?' Phil said.

'Wouldn't think of it,' the farmer said, pushing his wife's hand from his arm. 'Not a mite under four-five.'

'But four was the reserve price!'

'Yes, well, I'm sticking out for four-five. It's worth it to me, that place.'

'Well,' said Phil eventually, looking down, 'that's more than we wanted to spend really. I don't think we can go as high as that.'

Lucy stared at him as if he were the enemy now, and her eyes ached. 'Phil!' she cried; but he took no notice, and the two men stood there, poised against each other, and she was ranged somehow with the farmer's wife, who was weak in her pleading, a nonentity; she was discarded with the women who sit and wait. 'Phil, we can afford it!' she exclaimed, before he could come at her with his sideways warning look, his frown of distaste, 'Of course we can! Fancy making such a thing about five hundred pounds.' Her chin was up as she stared, challenging him; she felt the woman beside her shrink away, saw her lover flush up with his rare tense anger, but must press on now and risk everything between them. And all of a sudden, the tension was gone, as if they had been on a tight wire and, looking down, seen that it was only inches above the ground. The farmer was smiling at her with amused and fatherly affection, and taking no notice for the moment of Phil.

'You sleep on it,' he said, 'and we'll give it till tomorrow night, and you give us a ring. We'll be in after tea. I'm sticking at four-five, but I'll leave you the first refusal.'

'Thank you very much,' Phil said in his flat angry voice, all of him controlled.

And 'Oh, thank you!' cried Lucy, the tears standing full in her eyes, long hair escaping from its untidy knot and falling in strands. 'But have we got your address? And you're on the 'phone? Quick, Phil, give me the pen.' And she snatched the old felt pen as he brought it out of his pocket, fumbled in her bag for an old envelope and wrote upon it, when she had licked the used-up pen, their name and number. 'The address!' she laughed at them, 'of course we know the address! I believe it's emblazoned on my heart.'

The middle-aged couple, standing together in the room, apart from their friends, smiled tolerantly and watched them go.

Outside in the darkening windy street their anger licked between them, a rising flame, threatening as it flowered to char all that they had already built. Behind them, the house in which tranquillity would live was fading, the quiet rooms a mockery, the wide view a shared torment, the very calm and country peace that they were promised far too much to bear.

'What the hell d'you mean by bursting out like that?' Phil's voice was contemptuous, after they had walked a few yards in silence, and it was this that snicked at her like the end of a whip.

'Well, it's just ridiculous, pretending we can't afford it, niggling over a few hundred pounds when we'd agreed we'd spend about four thousand. It would have gone, if I hadn't said anything, it would have, and you would have let it, just for five hundred quid.' The tears were now streaming down her face, unchecked in the kind darkness. When she cried, she was like a child beating against some solid object that would not move for her; she sobbed first in frustration and then, as her fists hammering, her feet kicking, caused her pain, in the realisation that hurting him, she hurt herself. He hated to see her cry; she could feel his mounting irritation as he heard the sob in her voice; as if, by registering his disapproval, she could stop. Her tears flowed easily, as they had when, a child tormented by some bigger girl, she stood in a corner of the playground, laughed at because she had red hair; and yet, then, there had been no way out, while now she could check him, bring him back to her with a word, a simple gesture; she could say 'I'm sorry. I love you,' and he would turn, his face cleansed of all its anger. Only, this was impossible. Her lips formed around the words in the darkness, but her throat could emit no sound; there was still the mistrust, the wariness of the cornered child who could not accept the risk. So, she walked along beside him, feeling the feet of dark space between them, knowing that his continued silence meant that he considered her outburst unworthy of a reply. It would be useless to say any more about it now.

'Where are we going?' she asked eventually, daring a little to approach him.

'Well, there's still time to get to my parents. They won't be in bed yet, and they're expecting us. We'll get on a bus.'

'Supposing there isn't a bus?' She seized at a small hope and knew that her lack of rationality annoyed him further. Of course, there would be a bus. It was still, she had noticed as they left the pub, only just after nine. But to go to his parents' house tonight – the thought left her trapped and dismayed, a frail animal lured on by kindness to the waiting steel. It was always like going into a tunnel. One entered at one end of a weekend, travelled along separately and in the dark, groping now and then ineffectually one towards the other, and emerged at the other end dazzled by the ordinariness of one's own welcome life; Monday morning found one eagerly escaping, among strangers. All that subterfuge, that politeness, those pointless lies; and Phil was telling her bus times, hurrying her towards the stop at the end of the village street, and she seized his arm, trotting to keep up with him.

'No!' she cried, 'Not tonight, we can't!'

'What d'you mean? I thought we had it all arranged. They're expecting us.' He was still aloof.

'Oh, Phil, you know what I mean, it would be awful. Tomorrow, but not tonight.'

He was taken aback, knowing what she meant, loving her again for having pulled him back from his solitary rage, baffled though, as always, by her disrespect for plans.

'But they'll mind, if we don't turn up. There'll be a hell of a scene. Anyway, where could we stay? I don't fancy the roadside.' He took refuge in practical considerations; they had to stay somewhere, so it might as well be his parents' house. She was absurd, but he knew again that he loved her.

'Well, I don't know, there must be a hotel or a bed and breakfast place somewhere. We could ask.'

'I suppose so. But we haven't got much money.'

'Oh, we've got a cheque book, haven't we?' She was exasperated at his lack of ingenuity. 'You think of something, anyway, because I'm not going to your parents' tonight. We'll be interrogated as soon as we get there and shoved into separate beds, and I can't stand it.' He shivered, wanting sleep, warmth, protection. 'Anyway,' she concluded, 'it's your mother's birthday tomorrow, isn't it, and we haven't bought her a present, and we can't possibly get one tonight, and if we sneak out tomorrow morning to look for one, it'll look as if we've forgotten. Whereas, if we don't go till tomorrow, we can buy something on the way and turn up with it, and she'll be so pleased we remembered, she won't mind us turning up late.'

'Christ,' his hand covered his mouth, 'so it is. God, I'd completely forgotten. Yes, O.K., that does seem a better idea. Come on, we'll go and look for somewhere to stay.'

They set off down the road again, leaving the bus stop with its straggly queue, she obscurely uncomfortable with her ability to lead him through tortuous paths, unnoticing; walking companionably again, hand in hand and in step to search the village, they brooded separately upon the evening.

An hour later, they were still looking for a bed. In the village, they stood squashed together in a telephone box that smelt of old copper coins and Lucy heard, weakened by distance, Phil's mother's quick disapproving voice. Asking, always asking. Phil mumbled into the receiver, his breath misting the black plastic, the ends of his words inaudible; she took his hand and stroked the palm and the long fingers as he spoke and let him feel her weight against him, to say that they were doing the right thing.

'Ah, hell,' was all he said, when he put down the receiver, but he took her in his arms in the lighted kiosk and pressed his cheek down upon the top of her head, while they looked through their own reflections in the glass, out to the solid night. She fitted herself to him, hoping to feel the hard rising pressure in answer, through his jeans, but there was nothing but the weight of his tired head, his motionless hands. She had felt him waver, had heard the note in his voice when he made excuses to his mother and she interrupted. The weekend waited, only a short night away; already there was the tremor on the wire, the message of fear. Things would have to be changed, decisions made.

A man was waiting outside the kiosk, his face, pressed up suddenly white against the glass, blotting the vision they saw of themselves; and both jumped at the intrusion. Phil pushed open the heavy door with difficulty, to let her out into the street; the cold air after the staleness.

'Got no bed to go to, then?' The man mocked,

barging past into the kiosk, tongue sucking testily on his teeth. He glared as he closed the door; a hostile messenger.

'Just that, mate,' Phil said sharply in reply to the closed door. The simplest things the hardest to find. A bed for two lovers for the night. They tracked backwards and forwards across the village street, asking in pubs where the last customer stood at the bar, at the doors of houses where light still rimmed the curtains, if there were anywhere here, anywhere at all, where they could spend the night. But the village was closed against them, and the black winding road into the fens led only to barns and straw-stacks and mountains of sugar beet; they thought of the dour healthy faces of the farmers at the auction, their wives preparing for bed, setting the alarm clock for the morning, cream on their faces and bosoms pendulous in brushed nylon.

'Think of them all in bed with each other,' Lucy suggested, to cheer him. 'Doesn't it seem incongruous? All those couples who can't remember why they married each other, sitting there in bed, night after night.' But the thought did not seem to him funny, only macabre. He was dimly afraid, and hungry too. It was a long time since they had had those fish and chips, and he was a man who needed constant feeding, who grew instantly depressed if he saw no prospect of food.

'They're not going to let us in,' he said, and stopped walking with the weariness of it. 'This is Puritan country, that's the trouble. The ghost of Cromwell in every corner. We just don't look married, I suppose.'

She knew that unless she made a suggestion of some practical worth he would begin to hate her again for having brought him to this situation; but she had not known him long enough to tread carefully.

'Let's get a taxi,' she said.

'Yes, just look at all those taxis teeming around. I'd forgotten we were in Piccadilly Circus. God, Lucy. What's the time, anyway?'

They examined watches by the light of an uncurtained window. His said 10·50, hers 9·15.

'Why don't you get that watch mended?' It infuriated him that she should go on wearing it just because she liked the look of it. Machines, he thought, should work to simplify existence, not tie one in knots and make of life even more of a jungle than it was already.

'I expect because you'd have nothing left to carp about, if I did,' she said. 'You say that once a day, and it's bloody boring.'

'But I don't understand why you don't get it mended. It's irrational.'

'Well, since yours keeps such excellent time, I can't see why mine can't be purely decorative. Anyway, it's my watch, and it's none of your business.' But she thought, oh, God, here we go again, oh God produce a solution, let something turn up, because I love him and I can't cope. It was her belief that when one neared the abyss, something always happened to snatch one back from the edge; and thus, near-disasters could be almost enjoyable, since one knew, as things worsened, that fate would soon intervene. And then, the comfort after misery; the hot bath and the glass of whisky after the icy wait, the perfect lift after hours of hitch-hiking, harmony after stress, passion after a quarrel. The beautiful irony of life. And so, they could fight and tear each other, and then be so marvellous, loving and forgiving and laughing together at the fugitive fears that had dogged them, and it would all have been worth it. She knew he would call her perverse if she told him this, and the very straightness of him, in rejecting this game, pleased her all the more. Now, sure of herself – for, in the end, somewhere, somehow, they would find a bed – she called upon fate, God, the eye that looked down from the violet sky, and said: now; now, this is the moment, we have had enough of waiting, we now need satisfaction. At that moment, a large car came up the street, headlights full up and dazzling them, as if the driver had arrived so quickly from so far a place that he had not had time to notice that this place was uninhabited. The lights dipped, the car swung in to the side and the window was rolled down.

'There, what did I tell you?' Lucy shouted, scrambling already towards the car, clutching her tattered handbag.

'What? You didn't tell me anything! What are you doing?' Phil, catching her up with his long running stride, arrived at her side as she reached the car. In the darkness they both saw the pale face of a man peer out, the window rim reaching his mouth. 'Are you lost? Do you want a lift somewhere? I'm going down to the London road, through Frensham.'

'Fantastic!' cried Lucy, and tumbling already on to the back seat, pulled Phil in beside her. 'That's where we're going, too, only we couldn't seem to get there. We're looking for a hotel.'

'White Hart, Frensham,' the man said, as if a button had been pressed. And they drove away.

Once they were inside the hotel, the door of the bedroom shut behind them and all doubt eliminated, she threw herself down on her back on the spongy bed and exclaimed, 'Oh, wasn't this a stroke of luck! Just think, we might still have been wandering down that ghastly street, poking round that dead village till all hours. Oh, I knew something would turn up, and it did.'

He could have said that it was in that dead village that she wished so much to live, that the car's arrival had had merely a mathematical probability about it; but he was tired and there was the wide bed with the clean sheet turned down for them, so he threw his long body down beside hers and gently agreed, that they were the luckiest people, that fate smiled, the stars were in their right places, and that nothing could, for them, ever really go wrong.

'And it's a gorgeous room, really, isn't it?' she was saying, chin and lashes pointing to the ceiling where she lay close to him; for it had to be, to play its proper rôle, to keep the charmed circle intact. He got up on one elbow and looked around. It was big, yet somehow arid. Everything in it seemed designed to be appropriate to a bedroom, yet there were large gaps between everything, showing each object up as too big or too small, too plain or too ornate. Long curtains hung, hiding the windows and stifling sound; he breathed with difficulty, feeling that the windows were perhaps fakes, decorating a blank and impassable wall.

2

FELICITY RIDGLEY turned over and glanced at the
time, but not until she was fully awake did it occur
to her. For today the shallows of sleep teemed with
lesser thoughts, vaguer and more pleasant feelings.
Not until she had drunk two cups of tea, hooked up
her bra to contain falling breasts; not until she had
chosen the cashmere sweater and the skirt that toned,
made up her face, powder, a little eye-shadow, the
red bow of the thirties faded unintentionally now to
suit the sixties; not until she was already down in the
kitchen while the rest of the house still slept, did she
remember that it was her birthday. Odd, for she had

hardly forgotten during the last few weeks, hardly indeed spared herself a moment of the pain, the apprehension. She was fifty; it was a thought, like a prick upon the skin, the itch of a mosquito bite, that had forced itself upon her as she sat in the bath, or washed up, or paused for a moment before a shop window to be sure that all was well; she would be fifty, in a few days. Yet the date itself had not occurred to her. Surely it would be a day slipped in unnoticed by all except herself, a day like the last one of February that never happened, but had passed. A calendar hung in the kitchen and the day was indeed 25 September, her day. She had stood there a couple of days ago with a biro poised to write 'Philip here' on its blank space, to give herself something firm to be happy about, till he should arrive. She had not written 'My Birthday' as she had done as a child. The family would think it was there to remind them, but no, that was not true; it was that she had actually, for the moment, forgotten. She had wanted to forget. And neither had she written 'Andrew and Heather here' on that space two days earlier. They had been here two days. She wondered if they had noticed.

The day was fine, and everything with the first sharp gleams of sun through the kitchen window became easier. They would be able to take their glasses of beer out in the garden before lunch, and not get under her feet in the kitchen as she strode about, reaching, placing, tidying, stirring, preparing the meal that was to be her birthday lunch. She would be able to shoo them all outside again after lunch, and then she would potter among her things throughout the afternoon, counting them and polishing them and putting them away, ready for the next meal. There might be a play on the radio or a programme for people alone. She would switch it on in the breathless scrubbed privacy of her own kitchen and be pleased, remotely, that her family was around her. A cosiness, a refined pleasure. It was a feeling that remained from her children's infancy, induced by the sight of her husband busy and harmless at some useful job, of her small sons safe in their playpen, or later using a new toy, a carpentry set or a box of crayons, something constructive, in the way it was meant to be used. Noise, chaos, the misuse of property, her fears; she had in some measure passed them on to her sons. And the scheme of things, the safe plan and the ordered day, these were what took away the fear; she must love propriety, details. Tidied drawers of linen, pots of jam on a shelf, labelled. She must touch and tidy, imposing her order upon material existence, feeling the reassurance flow through her fingers and the healing of the terror reach her mind. As a little girl, she had had those rows of dolls, and had helped her mother tidy her work basket, her wool drawer, her beautiful button box wherein the buttons could be matched, and the intensity of that pleasure had become now the negation of pain. She could still remember the smell of that drawer of wool, high up in the polished tallboy, and the clink of the buttons to be sorted into sets, ready to be sewn on; but then, it had been a gratuitous joy, and now, she knew it, they all said it, or looked it, it was more like a compulsion. The present was like that, all anxiety, fear that was there like the flies in summer, in spite of the sticky flypaper. George was all right, going to work, coming back, kissing her when he remembered, pottering out into the garden for hours of the long summer evenings, snipping off the dead heads and pulling out weeds. Andrew was all right, although the wedding had been exhausting, and Heather's pregnancy and her confinement a strain on her nerves; Andrew had his job and his house not too far away, and Heather, whom she had dreaded, was kind and sensible, a considerate young woman, a good wife to her elder son. But Philip. Philip, the younger, the baby, the one she loved, the one who brought in bunches of wild flowers in a sticky hand, who cried at night and needed her, who had bad dreams and whose damp cheek was like petals under her stroking hand, who needed her, and in needing her created a new feeling which set him apart from the rest – Philip was maddening and brusque and unpredictable and did not come home for months at a time, made her worry, made her old. Made her fifty, without love, without hope. Today Philip was coming in time for lunch, and she began to worry in case it might be worse than last time even, and Monday might come with that sick, tired feeling and nothing to console her. Philip was coming for lunch, with Lucy.

'Why girls can't dress like girls, I don't know. And for Sunday lunch, too.' George, last time Lucy had been with them, deliberately held out the rapier point to his son.

And 'All you ever do,' Philip came back from the kitchen to say it, pausing on the threshold, 'all you ever do is criticise. That's all I ever hear. And now

28

it's Lucy. Honestly, I might as well buy a gramo-
phone record.'

And then there was herself, driven by her loyalty
to Phil, defending, always defending what she did
not know about, making herself foolish in his eyes.
'For God's sake, Mum,' he would say. 'Look, you've
made the point. For God's sake don't go *on.*'

Defending, smoothing it over, papering the cracks.
Disunity tired her; her aim, her comfort, was to have
them all there, agreeing with each other. It happened
rarely now that the boys were grown up, yet when
they raised their glasses at Christmas, when they all
laughed at the same television show, she felt that
quiet hum of achievement. They had all been such a
happy family, underneath. There had been picnics,
with thermoses of tea, and bridge rolls spread with
paste, family expeditions, family walks. Family
birthdays, and parcels at Christmas-time produced
after days of secrecy and scuffling in the attic, and
presents for herself, evidence of their love. Now
she thought, has Philip remembered my birthday?
If Philip has forgotten my birthday, I shall have
failed.

The thought must be erased. Briskly she laid out
coffee cups, plates, knives, butter, marmalade, spoons
and cereal packets, with the packet of wheatgerm at
George's place, because he seemed so often tired, and
a single plain yoghourt for herself. There were four
of them again, Heather here instead of Philip. At
lunch there would be six, and then there was the
baby, to be fed on Farex and hastily mopped and put
back in his pram, while they ate. The number had
grown, five people came to celebrate her birthday

with her, five to make up the family circle. Yet she was not happy.

Andrew came in, his arm went round her and he kissed her cheek. 'Happy birthday, Mum.' His eyes, unknown to her, flickered over the headlines of the morning paper. She did not kiss him but was busy, imperturbable, at the sink. His hand came out from behind his back and held out a packet, wrapped in tissue paper. His eyes met her look guiltily, he smiled and shifted his glance and went to help himself to cereal while she held it, turned it around in her hands, pleased with the homage and yet uncertain. She wanted to put it on one side and not open it. It was enough that he should have given it to her, that there was something, a token, wrapped up in tissue paper. She did not want to know what it was. It was soft and light. She put it down gingerly upon the breakfast table and drew her hands back from it.

'Go on, open it.' He stood there with his bowl of cornflakes, munching. 'It's from Heather and me and Jojo. Hope you like it.' He was watching her, he was a married man with the trepidation of a small boy in case she might not like it, his eyes wary over the lifted spoon.

'Do sit down, dear.' Her fingers groped in the soft paper and slipped off the ribbon. 'I don't know why you all eat as if you had to catch a train or something. Go on, darling, you'll give yourself indigestion.'

A long silk scarf slid from the paper, rippling out in front of her eyes, under her touch, something scarlet and purple and green with the vivid marks of the jungle, a beautiful thing that caught at the rough places on her fingers, that flashed its barbarism in

30

the sunlight, that sighed as it folded and slipped and evaded her. She wanted to pull down the blinds, and to fold it up in its paper and put it away in a drawer forever. With fear she faced him. 'It's lovely. Thank you so much, darling. How very kind of you.' Her hand flew up to pat her hair and smooth her face, then she placed a light hand on his shoulder and kissed him on the cheek. He bent his head to hers obediently, and went on crunching up his cornflakes as she touched his cheek with hers and made a kiss noise somewhere near his ear.

'I thought you'd like it. Heather chose it, actually.

'It's lovely,' she repeated, guessing in her pain at the girl's cruelty in choosing it. Her powder blue jersey, her tweed skirt, her make-up, her very self, were fading fast in the light of the brilliant silk.

'Put it on, Mum, won't you? It'd look good with that outfit.' He gestured with his spoon.

'Oh, no, not now, it'd be such a pity to spoil it. Wouldn't it? No, I'll keep it for best.' It was bright and rapid, her reply; she humoured him as if he were a little boy, and all of a sudden he felt it and flushed, for all his life his presents had been received like that, then put aside, whereas Philip – whatever Philip brought would be welcome, some scruffy twig of a plant would be put in a vase, some scribbled drawing pinned above the mantelpiece; and it had cost four pounds, that scarf. Four pounds for a scarf! It was Heather's fault, as it was her fault that he had been secretly shocked when she told him the price and yet had not dared to protest. And looking at it, where it lay graceful and gaudy upon the table, he knew all at once what his mother had felt; he looked from her to the beautiful, appalling thing, and was deeply ashamed. He sat down and poured his coffee and drank it in silence.

But she could not leave it alone, for her defences had been down and must be built up carefully, bit by bit, tested and tried.

'Look!' as soon as George came in, 'look what Andrew and Heather and Jojo have given me! Isn't it gorgeous, darling? Wasn't that kind of them? Andrew, it's lovely. Heather chose it, George. Wasn't that clever?'

'What a lovely scarf,' George looked at his son, surprised. 'Good choice. Good taste, Heather has. You'll look fine in that, darling, won't you?' He started to read the back of the cornflakes packet, and then remembered. 'Felicity, darling, I almost forgot.' Out of a drawer came another packet; she looked at his outstretched hand and even felt a little faint. The recognition she demanded was here, as it had been when the boys were children and George a young and conscientious husband. Yet she wanted it all pushed back into drawers and locked up, safe. She looked at him, almost pleading.

'Kitchen scissors,' he said. 'Come on, open it, love. You said you needed some, didn't you? I thought a good big pair would come in useful.'

She smiled her gratitude and relief, feeling the hard outlines of the scissors through the paper, and put the parcel down. There was no need to open it, no fear to be exorcised. They understood each other. It was he who leaned across to kiss her, out of habit, and then he smiled with satisfaction and sat down to his breakfast.

32

'What time's Philip coming?' The silence had lasted only seconds, the reassurance had flickered and was gone.

'Oh, I don't know. They never let me know. They just deign to turn up when it suits them. I only hope they'll be here in time for lunch, after all this.'

'I thought he said he was coming last night.'

'He was supposed to be. It was his idea. I don't know, I can't think why they can't stick to a plan. He rings up from the middle of nowhere with no proper excuse, and then expects us all to change our plans for him, keep meals waiting, keep beds aired. Oh, he'll turn up when he wants a bit of home comfort, all right. He'll be hungry enough when he gets here. They don't look after themselves.'

'Lucy coming too?' maliciously asked Andrew, who knew she was.

'Oh, yes. They don't seem to be capable of going anywhere without each other, these days.' She sighed, and Andrew smiled into his coffee cup.

'I rather liked Lucy,' George said.

'I thought you couldn't stand the way she dressed. I thought you said she was peculiar. And her hair, I remember you saying it was all over the place. Like a bird's nest. You certainly seem to change your mind fast enough.'

'Well, but I quite liked her. She seemed to have a mind of her own. More than that Philip's got, at any rate.'

Felicity drew her lips in as if she were reshaping her lipstick and moved around the table, tidying up around them, moving the marmalade jar, straighten-ing the knives, scratching at a tiny spot on the tablecloth with her nail. 'Well, do get on with your breakfast, it's almost ten o'clock, and I've got the lunch to get. I can't have breakfast going on till all hours, with a joint to get in the oven. Now, I wonder where Heather's got to?'

Andrew's head came up, to protect his wife, but at that moment Heather came in, the baby balanced on her hip, his small bare bottom and tiny prick dangling.

'Hallo, Heather.' George scraped his chair, as if to rise, but stayed where he was.

''Morning. I wondered if you'd got any spare cotton wool? I seem to be out of it. He was in an awful mess, absolutely covered in it, weren't you, love? Poor little boy. I'm sorry to be so long. Don't bother about breakfast for me, I'll just have a cup of coffee later on, if that's O.K. Oh, happy birthday,' she said to Felicity, seeing the scarf, 'I hope it's what you like. You can always change it, you know, if the colours aren't right or anything. I got it at Marshall's. We wouldn't be offended, would we, Andrew?'

'Thank you, dear, it's lovely. Now give me that baby, and come and eat your breakfast. I'll finish him off for you. Though how we'll get any lunch at this rate, I don't know. Breakfast just seems to get later and later, and I've still got the joint to get in.'

'Really,' said Heather, 'I don't want any. I'd be quite happy with just a—'

'I'll take him,' Andrew said, getting up laboriously, reaching for his son. 'You have some breakfast, darling, or some coffee or something. You sit down, Mum, and have a rest.'

She was gesturing against the possibility of rest,

scornful that he should even have thought of it. He stood there, her son Andrew, large and impassive, the baby very small in his arms with its heavy head drooping and violet eyes asquint, while plump dark Heather darted around them. Breakfast had become pointless; the toast cooled and grew leathery, the coffee had a grey skin; everyone was wishing that it were all over and that they were somewhere else. Heather sat down helplessly on the only empty chair, broke off a piece of dry toast and began to chew it. Felicity searched her mind for the right ritual phrase that would soothe them, the gesture that would make them all at peace. She gazed, saw her creation splintered, in pieces, felt all her work pointless; she fixed her gaze upon George, but he afforded her no help.

'Phil coming this morning?' Heather asked at last, as she mopped her lips after the coffee. This time, nobody answered. George read the paper, or stared at the headlines; Felicity, a little pucker between her brows, turned away to begin the washing up. The affirmation came only from Andrew, who nodded and stuck his lower lip out and raised his eyebrows at her. Once, she would have asked, 'Why, what on earth's the matter?' Only now, she had been three years a Ridgley, and she did not.

A long-haired tortoiseshell cat was lying in the sun upon the hotel porch as she stepped outside into the glittering chill of the September morning; its fur pricked out delicately against the light, it lay crouched between its paws and furled a pink tongue regularly down its forearm, back and forth. Lucy stopped to stroke it, giving it the rough rub behind the ear that would bring its moon face up to hers in ecstasy. The cat purred and stared for a moment and resumed its licking, as if it were the solid centre of a shifting universe; Lucy, poised above it, felt herself drawn down into the animal's aura of certainty, was blinded all at once by the sun that flashed up her arm and stung her face. She saw the golden hairs stand up on her own arm, each one separate as the cat's had been, she felt her own heavy mane swing down her cheek and saw the strands bright as piano wire before her eyes, the skin of her arm white, the wristwatch flashing gold. All was sharp, clear, visible. She thought, this is what I have done, what I am; I am able to see and judge; I can stand apart and see the bright strands. Today, something will happen. Inside the hotel, all was dark and cold, shielded from the morning. They had stood at the desk to give back the key and pay their bill and had known that the lie told was known already in every corner of the hotel. Frightened, Lucy had fled out into the sunshine, thinking of the sheets left upstairs in a wet and tangled mess, and the girls who tidied the rooms, and the Mr and Mrs scrawled late at night in the hotel book, hastily done and yet ineradicable, accusing her of her hypocrisy. She shuddered, still cold from the hall and the dark dining-room where they had sat on an island and eaten the platesful of fatty bacon and egg that had swum up out of the dimness, propelled by a careless hand. The taste of the coffee was still in her mouth, and the cloying feeling on her lips after eating fried egg. She fumbled about in her big handbag for cigarettes, found old paper handkerchiefs and screwed-up magazine cuttings, packets of pills, torn-off addresses, blunt used eyebrow pencils, old biros; all that jumble of things which she would hide from Philip and yet which was her, as surely as the fiery hair and the broken finger-nail and the body which he loved. The cigarette, found, drenched all other unwanted tastes, and she blew smoke out at the morning, a woman again, waiting for her husband in the temporary brilliance of the sun.

During the night, they had not mentioned the house. But now Phil came out through the porch, tucking his cheque book into the back pocket of his trousers, and asked, 'Well, what are we going to do about it?' and she was still close enough to the warm sleeping Philip of the night to know what he meant.

'Oh, let's ring them up and say yes!'

'They said, don't ring until this evening. We'll have to ring from my parents' house, I suppose.'

She was not daunted. 'We'll go out and ring from the pub. And nothing can really change between now and this evening if we don't want it to.'

Yet to Phil there was something missing. He saw them slip out, dial the number, arrange it all; but in his imagination he could not make the picture complete. He said, with a certain caution, as she smiled up at him, 'But we mustn't set our hearts on it too much, love.' It will be like this, he thought, seeing her sideways glance of scorn, hearing her call 'Why not?' as she willed him always to risk everything, as she slipped through his fingers like bright sand and danced ahead because she was irresponsible and he was the one to dry her tears when she slipped and fell, the one to foresee things and pay for them. He could not entrust himself so absurdly to a fate, he would never be the leaf on the wind; a shadow crossed his mind as he thought of the weight of that house, brick upon brick, tile upon tile, so many stone floor-flags, earth by the ton and measured in acres, that black solid earth; as if one day, like Sysiphus he would have to bear it upon his shoulders, straining uphill, while Lucy ran on, light and free. He took her hand and marched her now through the straggling groups in the market place, to find a bus. For yesterday they had stood together at the window of their house and looked out across the fields and the flat wild fen beyond, and her gaiety, her decisiveness had triumphed, and he knew that he could not do without her. Their thoughts ran underground, in silence, until the bus rolled into town along what he remembered as a rich green avenue of trees. Where the trees had been, there were now stumps. Lucy, her face averted from him so that her chin jutted, said, 'It's a bit like having known someone with beautiful long fingers, who's had them sawn off to the knuckle, so that just bone ends are left to stick up in that obscene way.' The street had been ugly enough, with its tatty hoardings and petrol stations strung with plastic flags, but once the trees had graced all that, giving dignity and strength to the earth which men had spoiled. But there was no hope in it now. The trees would sprout again next spring, but feebly, twigs like the hands of a thalidomide child, ugly and ridiculous. And now, as they came into town and there was no turning back, she felt heaviness descend, making her hands too unwieldy to lift from her lap, her face too drawn in to smile. Somewhere there was peace, somewhere their house in the stillness of the fens; the only source of goodness was remote now, and they travelled in the wrong direction. She glanced in fear at Phil, as if they might drown.

'Isn't it appalling?' he said. 'People must be insane.'

'I think people must be jealous of trees. I suppose they must feel better after chopping them down, cutting bits off, snipping them down to size.'

'But this – this castration.' He gestured feebly. 'I just have a complex, I suppose. But it makes me feel unsafe.'

The walk from the bus station to his parents' house was a good half-mile, and they walked fast, as if they did not want to risk contamination.

'God, how do people *live* here?'

'They just do. I just did, for seventeen years.'

'Yes, I know. Oh, I didn't want to be mean, but Phil, honestly, it's like a morgue. I can't believe that people eat and sleep and talk and make love here. Do they? Or do they just go through the motions, like making shadow pictures on a wall? I mean, it must affect you, I can feel it affecting me already, and I've only been here a couple of minutes.'

'It affects you all right,' he said. 'The traffic's got worse, though. Hey, I don't remember that house. Oh, it's been painted. Funny, it used to look quite different. I used to go to tea at that one on the corner sometimes. It belonged to some people called Willoughby. I was at school with the kid. We had to eat two bits of plain bread and butter, then two bits with jam, before we had any cake.' He laughed, 'I wonder if he's on a slimming course yet.'

'Phil, don't you mind? I mean, didn't you mind?'

'Hell, of course I minded. What d'you think? But nobody's past is unadulterated shit. You have to be a bit fond of the person you were, or there's no continuity. This place may be horrible, but in some sense it's me.' But he caught her glance and an inward shiver passed through him, the apprehension that today would be a battle in which Lucy's world would confront the old order, while he, who hardly existed, would be the battleground. Yet it was too late to go back. They walked together close and erect as scouts in enemy country, stiffened at the first whiff on the wind of fear.

Lucy said suddenly, 'God, Phil, your mother's present.'

Panic rose in him, but he said, 'Well, it's too late to go back now.'

'Aren't there any shops between here and there?'

'Only the sort you buy plastic chickens in. Oh, forget it. I'll get her something on Monday. She won't mind.' He saw himself and Andrew, little boys in their clean tee shirts, queuing up on their mother's birthday, to give her their presents. Andrew would have bought a present.

'It's ridiculous,' he told Lucy, 'all this fuss about birthdays. My mother's got a thing about it. She's always on about the dear dead days that never existed anyway. It makes me sick, actually.' He spoke loudly, daring the walls around to hear him blaspheme against the family ethic. 'Oh, darling, you shouldn't have bothered,' he heard her voice, the deliberate sham. 'Look, George, look what Phil's given me, and he made it all himself!' And the present, the package

40

tied with string, the babyish knots, the message inside, 'To Mummy with lots of love from Phil', the pathetic child's present that would be cradled and admired until he blushed with shame, because after all it was nothing, there was none of himself in it; the drawings that would hang on the wall, his simulation of childhood. Taught to give, forced to give, already a wary adult as he sat on the loo seat, six years old, refusing, refusing; so she wanted his shit, did she, tied with ribbons and a greetings card; she could do without.

'Here we are,' he said suddenly.

'It looks different from last time.'

'Yes, well, it was winter. Wasn't it? Snow, I seem to remember. Dad being sent out to shovel it away from the door, so that the postman wouldn't break his neck. And then there wasn't any post after all.'

She would not have recognised the house. Mesmerised by the sameness of these tidy places, these containing homes, their gardens, their driveways, their garages, she would have walked on past it, still swinging and striding and hiding behind her hair, so that she would not have to realise. But now he had dropped her hand, and they stood still and separate, facing the house. The windows, unsymmetrical, a bid for independence, stared down at them; blind, for there was as yet no face behind them. The square, pebble-dash front of the house gave no clue of life within. The front door, painted an acid green since their last visit, was shut firmly. Inside, people moved about and awaited their arrival, plotted even to destroy them, but yet the drop gathered, shimmered, had not yet fallen; they were safe, still, invisible, themselves for a moment as they stood outside and just looked; they could still have gone away. But the moment passed, the drop had fallen and splashed, the poise was altered and time moved on; for in the window of the house next door, a curtain twitched to one side, an old woman looked out, noting their arrival.

'There's old Mrs Fletcher looking out again.'

Lucy cried, 'I don't know how people can bear it. Always being watched from behind lace curtains, everybody knowing exactly what you're doing, taking down notes I expect, always nittering and nattering and grumbling about other people's behaviour. I just couldn't live without some sort of privacy. Real, I mean, mental privacy, not the privet hedge sort. God, it's so bourgeois, it's just unbelievable.' Her voice was high and edgy. The moment at which they could have gone away was past, and the present was like wading into cold water, not knowing what was under-foot.

'Oh, she's O.K.,' Phil said, 'just lonely, I should think. Must get pretty boring, sitting there all day.' He paused and waved briefly, and from behind the curtain a hand waved back.

'There's Philip.' Philip. Her hand went automatically to pull back the curtain, her lips felt their way around the word, saying it soundlessly. She never really got used to it.

He had come in, her own Philip, on that first day of a new life, in from the sunshine outside to the darkened room at her parents' house where she was playing the piano. It was the first page of that book of

42

simple Mozart pieces, and she skipped with her left hand because she could not be bothered to read the music, while her right hand knew the melody and rushed ahead, and through her mind the tune sang, 'Please come into the sun with me, please come into the sun with me, please sit down at my side, tell me you are . . . da da da da dah.' Then he came in, with her cousin Edward, and she was angry that they must have heard her appalling playing, her flippant, bad-tempered scampering through the practice hour.

'Why couldn't you have come in while I was drawing? Why couldn't you have seen me reading a book, and come up and asked what it was, so that I could exclaim, "Why, you like so-and-so too!" and we could have had a literary conversation?' she demanded silently of this strange young man, as she swung round on the piano stool, glaring at them, because they had pushed the door wide open and let in the blinding summer light, and she was at a disadvantage. He was pale and dark-eyed, this young man her cousin had brought in, his cheeks bony above his high collar, eyebrows uneven and tufted, hair a matt black, like fur on the narrow scalp, long side-whiskers narrowing his face to extreme thinness. His eyes, brilliant as though with tears, large and perhaps myopic.

'Go on,' he said. 'Please go on playing.'

'But I play so badly. I can't play the piano, not really.' I am not like this, there are dozens of things I do well; this is only what my parents expect of me. But he smiled, and under the slight moustache was the most tender mouth, laughing at her.

'It sounds so good,' he said, 'when you stand

outside a house and hear someone playing the piano. Especially on such a hot, silent afternoon. You have to stand still and listen, and you can't move on till the person who's playing wants you to. Really, I stood outside and stared at the wistaria for ten minutes, and I couldn't move until you played that last chord.' His fingers hovered over the music sheet, descended on the chord.

'But I played it wrong.'

'I know. You invented the left-hand notes. It should have sounded – like that.' His thin fingers came down upon the notes, stroking over the keys of the piano until they found their right place. 'But you played it – like *that*.' And he played her chord, pulling a face of pain. 'Still,' he said, 'it let me know there was a person of character inside, at least. Someone who wouldn't let herself be dictated to by an old, dead composer. So I came out of my spell and came in here.' He hovered behind her, his eyes scanning the page and his fingers above the notes as if he longed to play more. He was so close that she could smell the stuff of his coat, see the individual black hairs upon his cheek. She was silent, sitting there before him, docile as a pupil, not daring to move; and Edward had stood apart so that she was aware of his disapproval, Edward stood there shifting about and clearing his throat. But it was no use, after that, for anybody to disapprove.

The world had been without boundaries; now, it was smaller than herself. It had been so large, so limitless; now, it was like a walnut, right inside her head. There was nobody else who knew it. Her days had wound themselves up tight, lay curled inside her, all her memories put away, all her friends there in her mind. She was a stranger now to her own past, an old woman who had once been young, the last survivor, arbitrarily she felt, of a generation that was dead, left alone by the boys who had died in the first war and the men who had died in the second, by the women who had died giving birth, or in far away places where the sun had burned them to an early desiccation, who had vanished with no trace. For in the old people who stood in the shops now, and shuffled down the street, she recognised nothing of herself. Lovers, friends, relations had gone; Philip had gone; the old who were left were null and dumb and had always been old; they were nothing to do with her life. But a rare feeling assaulted her out of her own youth when she saw those two in the drive of the house next door. Philip, young Phil Ridgley nearly grown-up, and the girl with a look of scorn and the russet hair. To talk to them might be enough. Otherwise there were only the budgerigar and her faded cards, the trappings of age. One could ring them up, invite them over. The telephone sat upon its rest, used only once a week, for ordering the groceries. Her voice would sound strangely in the house next door, when they picked up the receiver. They would look at each other and say 'The old lady next door inviting us for tea?' and would ask 'Whatever for?', Phil forgetting his visits to her as a little boy, the girl not knowing, thinking it all a bore. She thought, I am nearly eighty, that in their eyes is enough, there is no point in telling them what I was. The intruding sun made her eyes water behind the glasses, she turned her head away. The house next door was full, hers was empty. There was no reason in it. Life embraced the young, tolerated the middle-aged, did not want to know about the old. 'But after all,' she said, 'you have nothing to lose. You may risk anything. There is nothing left to lose.' It seemed to be untrue. There was always one's vision of oneself to lose, one's myth, one's version of what it all had been; at eighty, this is too much to risk, where at twenty anything could have been changed, rejected or altered. 'But one must accept,' she told herself. 'One must risk the rejection, the final blow.' She saw herself prone at the edge of the sea, lapped by waves, now gentle, now rough; soon, the biggest would carry her off and gently she would be lifted from the firm ground, wrapped, borne higher, carried away unresisting. One only drowned if one resisted. Yes, if she approached them, they would try her and not turn away, for there was something in that child's stance, something of her arrogance, her innocence, her unfairness, her capacity for love, there was some-thing in that thin young man; they held adventure in their eyes, they knew perhaps what they were doing, they were children and yet she recognised them.

'I'll ask them. At four o'clock I shall ring them up. Not for tea – nobody asks them for tea any more. A drink, that's what they would like. Drop round for a drink. Or drop in? Or drop by?' Excitement rose in her; her old hands with their freckles and their blunt nails trembled as she lowered her lunch-time egg into its frothing water. The sherry bottle stood in the kitchen cupboard, untouched since last Boxing Day, when she had given some to the postman. Now she fetched it and stood it upon the table in the sitting-room, so that she should not have the cowardice to put it away untouched. The yellow label caught her eye as she cracked the top off her egg and ate her solitary lunch at the polished table in the window with the lace cloth and the cyclamen in its pot and the dark stain where her Philip had once put down his pipe. It was a long time since she had taken a risk, and she laughed quietly, thinking: Today something will change. By tonight, all will not be the same.

'But what is it you want, Helena?' Her mother always asked it, faced with that dreaminess, that discontent that had been hers.

'I don't really know.'

What had happened to Edward? A black bullet split his yellow skull. A young man who had played good cricket and got into some trouble or other at Oxford, he had been just one of them. She had not known where Philip was, or if he would ever come back again. Meanwhile she moved about her parents' house, wrote poems, watered pot plants, played with one finger on the piano the nostalgic songs of the day. The rooms around her were vast and dark, full of furniture. The garden stretched around her and seemed to keep people out, the newspapers lay about in piles, headline upon headline, the world was busy, absorbed, all except herself.

'I know what I'll do,' she said, eventually, 'I'll go to London.' He was there, as she had expected, he had not joined up and had no wish to do so, he was the only person in the world who was not going to talk about patriotism and doing one's bit; and he

simply walked into a restaurant where she was din-
ing with her godfather one night and told her that
the world was in a state of hysteria.

'But haven't they got to be fought?' she asked.
'Surely someone has to stop them.'

'Stop what? Stop the politicians. Ask any German
soldier how he feels about having his head shot in,
and he'll agree with your poor cousin.'

'Oh! So you aren't going? How very unfashionable.'

'Yes, isn't it? But I've got something wrong with
one of my lungs, anyway, so I wouldn't be much use.
I couldn't even run very fast in the wrong direction.'
He coughed and spluttered, to prove it. Her godfather paid the bill, and told her mother later that he
was not a desirable young man. 'Ill health and no
feelings for a man's duty' the phrase ran in her
mother's letter, and she laughed aloud, 'Unsound in
wind and limb, Philip, you've failed the veterinary
test and come up as an unpromising outsider. Shall I
write back and tell her an ill-winded son-in-law's
better than a dead one? Trouble is, she wouldn't
agree. All the best people are dead these days, accord-
ing to my mother. It's a positive sin to be alive.'

'Don't be flippant!' he called from the next room.
'You've caught it from me far too quickly. Write her
something soothing, for goodness sake.' For by now,
she had already promised to marry him as soon as his
divorce came through. There was so much chanting
and singing and weeping, that year, it seemed, so
many posters and songs and crowds of people and
bulletins from the front and news from the government, and in the middle of it all, there they were,

48

quite still, their eyes fixed upon each other, in a small room. 'I know what I want now,' she said.

Ten to one. Twenty more minutes for the joint, perhaps, that means we'll eat at a quarter past, the potatoes must go on now, and I must put the pie in on the lower shelf. The door slammed and she straightened up abruptly, a hand to her back where the pain had persisted since Philip was born, her cheeks unusually flushed, she felt.

'Oh, *there* you are.' She knew the irritability showed, and that it jarred instantly upon her son, making him recoil. 'Darling, how are you? Come on in, both of you. Where on earth have you been?'

'Been?'

'Well, you did say you were coming last night.' He stood there still framed in the doorway, a young warrior scenting danger.

'But I rang up.'

'Well, yes, at about ten o'clock at night. When we'd been expecting you to dinner. We were wondering what on earth had happened to you.'

'I didn't say we were coming for dinner, did I? Lucy, did I say we were going for dinner?'

'Look, it's the normal thing to have dinner where you stay the night. It's normal to turn up a few hours earlier than ten o'clock. It's common politeness. It's time you learned some manners, if you ask me. We were wondering what on earth had happened.'

'Well, I didn't turn up at ten o'clock. I telephoned at ten o'clock. I turned up at – what is it? – ten minutes to one. And nothing happened to me. I'm here.'

'Philip!'

'Well. . .'

'Darling, you must be tired. Thank goodness you're here at last, anyway. Oh, Lucy, what you must think of us, keeping you standing on the doorstep like this. Come on in, both of you.'

Andrew lurked in the hall, mouthing 'Birthday!'

'Happy birthday, Mum, anyway. I'm sorry if we had you worried.' He leaned forward, aimed his kiss. She clutched him, delicately placed her cheek against his for a simulated kiss that rejected him more squarely, he felt, than a blow across the mouth. He had made a wrong move to start with, and now there was no saving him.

'Mum, I haven't got your present yet, but it's coming. On Monday.'

'Darling, there's no need. . .'

'What is it?' said Andrew.

'Well, I wasn't sure what she'd like, I haven't exactly. . . . I wondered, Mum, what you really wanted. I mean, there was no point getting something you didn't.'

'Oh, Phil, darling, you don't have to go buying me presents. Wasting your money. And anyway, what's a birthday? Oh, I don't expect you boys to remember.' He was turning away, already disgusted. She floundered, groping through her own nervousness.

'I remembered, actually. Oh, forget it. What I really came to tell you is that Lucy and I are getting married.'

There must have been a dozen other ways she could have heard it; but the words came out by them-

50

selves, raw and unconcealed, as if he had no thought
of sparing her.

'Philip.'

'Fantastic, Phil. When?'

'Philip.' She said it again, pleading, saw his face
all hostility as if it waited for attack; she held
out an arm awkwardly to him, and he took her
hand. For the second time that day, she was shocked
out of herself by something unplanned and un-
familiar, and for the second time did not know
what to do, but simply wanted to go away and
hide.

'What's all this?' George was coming into the hall,
in his fawn cardigan, with his rounded old man's
back, his dark red face questing from side to side, to
find out.

'Dad, we're getting married. We've decided to get
married.'

'Get married?'

'Yeah.'

'What —' He was surely about to say, What d'you
want to do that for? and had checked himself. 'Oh,
yes, I see. Well, that sounds like good news. Well,
what d'you say to that, Felicity?'

He was the one who was mad. She looked across
at Phil, saw his blank face, his outrage on her behalf,
that she should live with this barbarian; and Phil put
an arm round her shoulders, squeezing her up to him
with his hand, touched her easily, as if it were easy
now for him to comfort those who were hurt; he who
had always shied away from affection. She was able
to reassert herself and find words. 'How lovely,
darling. Lucy, my dear, how lovely. Oh, you are a

dark horse, Phil. Tell me, when will the wedding be? What are your plans?'

He had dropped his arm from her shoulder and shrank back – she had erred again; she turned away her face in humiliation. There was no way to play this game, no way at all, no possibility of being herself and being accepted, no way of feeling and not being attacked.

'Oh, we haven't decided yet. The date didn't seem to us to be the most important thing.'

'No, no, of course not. I didn't mean it was. I just —'

'How are you going to manage?' George stepped in, all unaware.

'Manage?'

'Well, you're still a student, aren't you. I don't imagine you'll be giving that up to take a job.'

'No.'

'And I don't imagine they'll increase your grant. For the privilege of taking a wife. If I may say so, Lucy.'

'Oh, God.' Felicity trembled, feeling the air full of foreboding, knowing what would happen. 'Oh, Christ,' Phil said, 'I've only just got here, you never even ask me how I am. I've only just this minute arrived, and I've just told you about the most important thing in my life and all you can talk about is money. Oh, Christ, what a scene.'

'Philip, will you kindly not swear at me?'

'Oh, George,' she pleaded, begging for her day back, her hour, her remnant of a birthday. 'Darling, couldn't we talk about this later? It's all been a bit sudden, hasn't it? I'm sure it can all be worked out.

52

After all, he's not going to be a student forever, and I'm sure he can get a good job when he comes down from the university, and then I expect they can get married, and everything will work out.'

'What the fuck do you think you're saying?' He stood there, rigid, opposed, his eyes hating her, and the ugly words echoed and re-echoed, beating upon her ears, forcing her to believe them. She gave a little cry of protest, and fled from him into the dining-room.

She sobbed at the sideboard, waiting to hear George come in, and felt him stand there awkwardly beside her.

'Oh George, I don't know why you always have to be so hard on Philip.'

'Hard on him? What are you talking about? He's just said the most disgusting things to you, and I will not have it. That boy needs teaching a lesson. He hasn't got the manners of a navvy, and he's not getting away with that sort of language in my house, I can tell you. Hard on him! You must be out of your mind.' Again and again, it struck at him, when they were alone and against each other, the unjustness of her picture of him. She drew pictures of hostile strangers and held them up to him, each one with a placard, 'This is you.'

'Well, you didn't have to bring the money question up at that moment, did you?'

'Well, no, perhaps not. But he's got to think about it sooner or later, and I should say sooner than later. I mean, young people seem to think it's going to drop from heaven, these days.'

'But you could have waited. To say all that. Oh,

dear, and I did so want it to be a peaceful, family day. After all, it is my – but I know I shouldn't go on about it.'

'Your birthday.' He said it with a touch of the hardness he had shown to Philip, a quality he usually tried to conceal from her. She was so delicate, things hurt her so. He trod carefully round the house in his Marks and Spencer slippers, trotted down the garden like a good dog to potter and snip, asked her tenderly how her day had been when she had been out shopping and was tired. He was a peace-loving man, a peacemaker, a tranquil spirit in a time of unrest. He was annoyed with her now, for not having perceived it. Philip had turned his rough side up to the world, so that he was for a moment like a stone with the worms showing underneath; but it was Felicity who had looked underneath and judged him.

And she in turn remembered the touch of her son, that had driven back her fear. All those masked men who hung about the house, waiting to break in and wreck and steal, had been driven away for a while by his groping to find her hand, and hold it. George would not have done that, neither would Andrew. 'No, we aren't a demonstrative family,' she had told friends and neighbours. 'After all, if people really love each other, really get on, there's no need to hug and maul each other about, is there? No, we keep ourselves to ourselves, as you might say.' In other houses, there were children who rushed into rooms and tumbled their parents about, little boys who were allowed to kiss their mothers when they liked. George had always thought it unnecessary.

'You've always been hard on him,' she said.

'Now that is completely untrue. You do distort things so, Felicity. Now, when have I been hard on Philip?'

'Oh, it's me who exaggerates, is it? I like that.'

He sighed. Always, when they quarrelled, she became so ungrammatical, so illogical. She had no real weapons.

'When?' he said. 'Just tell me. When have I been hard on Philip? Just tell me some occasions. Some instances. Go on. You say I've been hard on him.'

'Oh,' she felt exhausted, felt the tears group again behind her eyes and wait to rush. 'I don't know. You don't expect me to remember everything in detail, do you? It's just that all his life you've picked on him. Criticised him. Compared him with Andrew. Made him feel inferior.' She spoke the words just as they occurred to her, not knowing whether or not they were true. What did it matter what one's weapons were, as long as one defended oneself? When he picked his way so pedantically, like a judge, like a prosecutor, forcing her to give evidence, remember dates, produce an alibi and recognise Exhibit A. He terrified her, and she ran backwards, lashing out. The only way was to hurt him, until he stopped. It was like not knowing if there was enough for dinner in the fridge, like people arriving, like being asked a question in class and not knowing the answer. When the masked men came to the door and banged upon it, they would want an answer, or they would push past her and invade the house.

'Well, if you hadn't spoilt him so absurdly, I might not have had to be hard on him. If I ever have been hard on him. Ever since he was a kid, he's had his own way. And now look at him. Conceited, self-opinionated, scruffy, immoral, filthy clothes, thoroughly proud of himself, filthy language – and in front of his parents – no proper considerations about his future. He's twenty-one, damn it, he ought to be thinking about a career, not mooning around about getting married. Married! What young man in his senses wants to get married at twenty-one? When I was his age, all I wanted was to see the world, get around a bit, try my strength, rough it a bit. Find my feet in the world. Be a man among men. Not get married!' He spoke so enthusiastically, warming to his story, enjoying the vision of himself so uncritically, that he gave himself away. She stood there beside the table they had bought together twenty-five years ago, and looked at him across the gulf. What was one to do? She loved him, in her way; he loved her, in his. The rancour was part of them, an iron band sunk deep in an old tree.

'Well, I didn't even meet you until I was nearly thirty,' he said, to save himself, and she nodded, the tears still in her eyes.

'Let's have a drink and go out in the garden with the children,' he said, tired of the situation. 'It's a lovely day, and after all, it is your birthday. We ought to have some sort of celebration.'

Then there was Andrew, in the hall, all carefulness in case something might break. She handed him the bottle of light ale, and he followed her. The glasses clinked on the tray, and outside there was sunlight. She saw Phil and his girl flopped on the lawn, where the grass was not yet cut, and she stepped towards them through the back door and carefully across the uneven lawn, balancing on her heels. Phil lay on his stomach, partly hidden, his wild dark hair like a cap of fur, the skin of a beast that had roamed mountains in central Asia. The toe of one foot balanced on the heel of the other. He was holding out something to Lucy, who sat back on her heels and looked at him, her face invisible behind that mass of hair. He was eating toadstools, or that was how it seemed, and she wanted to take him by the shoulders and shake him and force him to be more ordinary, to explain himself to her. He did not fit in any more, he had grown away. It was like the day she went to collect him from his prep school, and he had looked out of the window with a knot of other boys clustering behind him, and had seen her and refused to recognise her. The other little boys had waved to their mothers and Phil had stayed leaning against the sill, staring, his arms folded, while she stood and died in the drive.

The ones you loved did not love you; thus it had been all her life. Her father sat in his armchair by the fire and scowled at her stupidity. Young men glided past, sleekly black and white as cats, in the arms of other girls, girls with pouting lips and coils of hair and knees like water lilies, and she stood against the wall, waiting. The ones she followed with her eyes went on, and out of sight. To be with George, at last, was like being wrapped in a proud cloak, to step down a street at last in public. He had always been gentle, considerate. Yet when she unwrapped him, under the silky tissue paper was a hard, strange stone. She snapped the box shut and put it away in her drawer, and began to placate him. That was the birth of fear; she fled from his eyes and watched the kitchen clock for the moment at which he must leave for work, she invited neighbours in, they bought a television, she was always busy, and then tired. His face became the face of the invader, and at last he was everywhere, her fear was that she might come upon him unexpectedly, in the street, the shopping centre, the church hall; he might come up to her and make her turn suddenly and ask her what she was doing, with that note in his voice, that sarcasm; and she would look up, flustered, to face him, with no explanation upon her lips. So it was better to stay in, to walk backwards and forwards in her own kitchen, for there at least, if he came upon her, she would know who he was. The kitchen drawers, the tidily stacked sheets with their crisp corners in the airing cupboard were talismans against him, for they were solid, and existed. They lived together, inside their house, inside their marriage, and the days became weeks, weeks months, months years, and with this passing time, that nobody could stop and nobody account for, grew her fear.

Lucy standing there silently felt her lover begin to tremble, and she moved her hand in his, gripping his fingers.

'What the fuck do you think you're saying?' It was too late to recant. The mother ran, like a hen squawking.

'Philip, will you kindly remember where you are? Will you kindly go and apologise to your mother at once? We will discuss this later.' Never angry, never shouting. Cold and slow. Measured words, twist the screw in slowly, never at a loss for words. Phil was

58

looking steadily at his father across the hall, and she knew that they had always hated each other.

'You seem to have forgotten about Grandad's money. If we have to talk about money, I'd better remind you.'

'Well, you certainly needn't think you're getting your hands on that. I'm your trustee, remember.'

'I'm twenty-one.'

'Well, I would never have thought it from your behaviour. I can't say I see any signs of maturity. Now, will you please go and apologise to your mother.'

'For what?'

'For using disgusting language. For being rude, offensive and thoroughly inconsiderate. And on her birthday, too. You may get away with this sort of behaviour among your student friends, but you're not getting away with it here.'

'Dad, I never got away with a single thing here. Not even with being myself.'

'I don't know what you're talking about. I don't understand a thing you say.' He turned away and spoke to Lucy, 'We don't really mean it, you know. Our bark is worse than our bite, you might say. Oh, but I don't suppose there ever was a happy family without a bit of friction. I expect yours is the same.'

'Yes,' she said. He stared at them both abstractedly for a moment. 'Well, I'd better go and comfort Felicity. And Philip, I'd just go and say sorry, if I were you. You know what it means to her. And it's not quite on, you know, using that sort of language in front of her. I know you'll understand.' And he vanished, closing the door behind him.

Lucy heard him say, almost in a whisper, 'Oh, you bastard'; felt him fidget and grope in his helplessness, saw a young animal in a corral that kicked down its fences and stared out, frightened, at a great expanse. His hands played with the fringed ends of the mat on the hall table, he was looking past her in his confusion. Andrew came up the hall.

'Well, you could have managed that a bit better, couldn't you? Hallo, Lucy, nice to see you. Oh, it's great news, congratulations. Are you coming in?'

'Managed it?' Phil was lost still. 'Yes, I suppose I could have managed it a bit better. Everybody else seems to. But hell, why should I have to manage it? Why can't I just tell them I'm getting married, like any normal person? Why've we always got to skulk around and lay our little plans and warn people in case their delicate sensibilities might be hurt by our so much as existing?' He scratched his rough hair, gestured with one hand. 'I'm sick of it, I don't see why the hell I should creep about and pretend to be charming and bring birthday presents and everything just because they're expected of me. I've had it, I'm twenty-one, I'm grown-up, for Christ's sake. I don't understand you, Andrew.'

'Oh, God,' said Andrew, 'don't start bursting out at me. No, it's just that some ways of doing things upset them. You know they do. And you're not exactly here often. I should have thought you could afford to be reasonable about them while you are here. And it is Ma's birthday, after all.'

'Ma's fucking birthday.'

'Oh, Phil, come off it.'

'Look,' he said, 'I didn't want to get across them. I just said we were getting married, and they came down on me like a ton of bricks. I mean, what did they say when you got married? What would you have done if you'd been me? Sat there smiling when they said you could fucking well get married when you'd got your fucking degree and respectable job so that you could keep your wife in the turquoise moquette three-piece suite to which she was accustomed? No, when you say you're getting married everyone says lovely, what a lovely idea, go ahead, boy, get right in there. It's just different when it's you, isn't it?'

'Well, I was qualified.'

'Well qualified for the bridal bed. Splendid equipment you've got, son, beautiful box of tricks.'

'Oh, shut up. Look, are you coming in? I'm sure Lucy doesn't want to spend the whole day listening to your nonsense in the hall.'

'Let's go in, love,' she said. 'Come on. It doesn't matter.'

'Look, Phil,' Andrew said, 'I want to ask you something. Look, will you either be nice to them or go away? Today, I mean. Because the scene in this house is quite bad enough without you making it worse. Mum's fifty today. Well, she doesn't like it. And it's not easy for us, you know, being here, especially for Heather. But we thought it would cheer her up, seeing the baby and all. But what really cheers her up is seeing you. You know what she's written on that calendar for today? "Phil here". Just that. Nothing about her birthday, nothing about us. Just "Phil here" as if she was a little girl

looking forward to a treat. No, I'm not jealous or anything, after all, it's always been like that, hasn't it,
she'd never write "Andrew here" in a month of
Sundays. But if you're going to stick around, you can
bloody well be nice to her. To both of them.'

'But they aren't nice to me.' He dropped into a
chair and heard in the next room the sound of someone crying.

'Oh, Phil, they've been bloody good to us. You've
got to admit it.'

'That birthday business. That's just tyrannical.'

'But why? What's so odd about celebrating one's
mother's birthday?'

'Enforced celebration?'

'No, voluntary, of course.'

'But don't you remember, when we were younger,
being lined up with the presents we'd been made to
buy? Powder from Andrew, soap from Phil? How
clever of you, darlings, just what I wanted? Dad
smirking because he'd remembered in time to take it
out of our pocket money? And hours and days sweat-
ing over those birthday cards with our little paint
boxes and our stubby little brushes, keeping it all a
secret? With them splitting their sides in the next
room, because we were so cute?'

'No, I don't. I remember enjoying it. Going off with
you and Dad to choose presents, wrapping them up
and giving her a surprise. And we enjoyed watching
her open them almost as much as if we'd been getting
presents ourselves. I remember you in particular, you
getting all excited about it, wanting to give them to
her before breakfast.'

'You don't remember any such thing. You've just

62

been indoctrinated. In this family, if something doesn't fit in with the image, it just gets neatly chopped about and touched up until it's fit to go into the archives.'

The dining-room door swung open, the murmuring beyond them silenced; a voice called clearly from within. 'Are you in there, boys? If you'd all go out into the garden, I'll pass you out some drinks. Beer for everybody all right? Oh, Heather likes a bitter lemon, doesn't she? Oh, thank you, darling, yes would you take the tray?'

Philip faced Andrew at a few inches distance in the passage, 'See what I mean?' They followed out into the patchy sunlit garden; Heather came downstairs with the baby, greeted them briefly and arranged Jojo in the pram under a tree; Phil and Lucy lit cigarettes and sprawled on the grass; Andrew picked up a croquet mallet and stood idly swinging it, glancing occasionally towards his brother as if puzzled by something he had not yet understood.

'Phil,' Lucy said, the smoke in her nose and mouth.

'Yes?'

'It's not really such a battle, is it? You did sound bitter, just now. I'd no idea.'

'I felt it.' He bit off a stalk of grass. 'It just all came out suddenly, like being sick. It's odd, he simply won't admit it, will he? He simply won't remember.'

'What?'

'What it was like. That it was no bed of roses. No sweetness and light. But hell, he can't remember it like that, he's older than me, he must remember. Otherwise he's somebody else, not my brother at all. We were kids together, and now he's saying he liked

it, queueing up to hand over those presents in our
cute little matching shirts and pants.'

'People remember things differently.'

'Yes, but one of them must be right. I mean, one
of us. We saw the same things, felt the same things
happen. We were both there. And the point is, this
weekend, today, before we get married, well I can't
get free of my past if I don't understand it, and I
can't understand it if he's there contradicting me all
the time, can I? I mean, there are things, things
Andrew would deny. Which, for me, he'll have to
accept, have to remember. I've got to make him
admit them, before we go. Because, otherwise, there's
no reality. No me. D'you see?'

She looked at him and said nothing. The world
turned around them slowly, as it had outside that old
house in the middle of the fen. There were still those
open skies, and the clouds, turning and turning. She
had eyes of amber in the light, gold speckled with
darkness, as if dust had caught in them and stayed.
She looked at him through her hair, that fell glance
through the bright strands that wound him towards
her, trapped him in her shade. She sat now with her
hands open on her lap, as if everything had just
fallen into them; and it was he who lay on those
hands, small and shrunken, turned upward to the
light. He wanted to go and lay his head down at her
feet in the grass, and rest, but the bright watchful
look warned him that when he did she would gaze
out over him in triumph, the priestess with the
acolyte at her knees. The garden was dappled with
September. Yellow apples lay in the long grass by
the fence, yellow leaves floated singly through the

air, coins dropping through water; the grass was wet, the smell of the earth good, even here, where it was so put upon; the speckled air full of dust dancing. There was leaf mould and fungus buried, dead damp things reeked and rotted, fruit turned bruised sides to the ground and became earth. It would be easy to lie under a tree throughout nights of cold clarity and days of musk, to lie under the chrysanthemums and breathe only their acridity, easy to turn all scars and bruises down towards the earth until flesh became earth and all mingled and rotted and sank under the leaves. Higher than the earth were shelves with things upon them, letters half-written upon a table, hands clasping knives and forks above a loaded plate; higher, the air became dry with hurry. To lie with the earth, and breathe the damp, and eat toadstools, the little ones that grew by the fence. Phil's mother had once cooked him a caterpillar in his plate of cauliflower. She said, eat it up, it's only made of cauliflower. How can a caterpillar be made of cauli-flower, I asked, it couldn't run if it was only made of cauliflower. She said, because all it eats is cauliflower. I said, but there must be something, a little some-thing, there before. A bit of caterpillar, before it eats. And I cut it in half to see, and ate half. She said I was disgusting. He pulled up one of the little fungi, stretching a long arm to reach it, and bit its head off and chewed slowly.

'They're probably poison,' Lucy said, watching him.

'In that case, will I die?'

'You'll probably only get a stomach ache. But the French eat lots of weird little mushrooms.'

He swallowed, and paused a moment. 'This is my body, which is given for thee. Take and eat this, in remembrance of me.'

'Phil!'

'Go on,' he insisted. 'Take it. Please.'

She obeyed, staring out at him, wary as a cat in the bushes. Felicity Ridgley came towards them, swaying on her heels across the uneven grass, carrying her tray, Andrew following with a bottle. 'Whatever are you up to? For heaven's sake, what are you doing? Trying to poison yourselves with those things? I've no idea whether they're toadstools or mushrooms. If you're hungry, here's a tin of cheese biscuits. Really, you'd think you'd have more sense at your age than to go eating stuff like that. Philip, really.'

They looked up at her. There seemed to be tear stains around her eyes, tiny riverbeds, in which tears habitually ran, recently watered. Her face was still pink and white, streaky. She had been a long time in the dining-room.

'I'm sorry, Ma,' Phil said, 'about what happened earlier. I should have told you differently, I suppose.'

'Oh, that's all right, darling. It was just a bit of a shock, that's all.'

'Well, I'm sorry. I'm sorry I was rude.'

She made a faint click with her teeth and inclined her head to one side, as if she did not know what to say. Lucy, who still held the tiny mushroom with its long stalk between her fingers, put it away in the pocket of her jacket.

How time passes, was what she thought as she saw Philip and Lucy from her bedroom window, the boy's long body in the grass, the girl crouched somehow, as if to spring. That boy, that man, was the child who last week had run into the hall and then hesitated on the threshold of her sitting-room, remembering that he had been told not to rush into places like that. But the passing of time was part of her now; there was no real surprise left in noticing that others had grown and changed, while she had not. Tall weeds grew around her house, imprisoning her, dropping their long shadows against the window. A tree tapped when she tried to sleep. There was a round white box in the drawer beside her bed and her old fingers shook as they held it, to prise open the lid and take out one more pill. The eyes of her house turned towards the life of the Ridgleys, next door. 'She's going out again, and she's slammed the door. Now she's looking about, to see if anyone heard. He's in the garden, he's always in the garden, I don't think he dares go into the house. Yesterday she cleared out the entire kitchen again. So many jam pots, you wouldn't believe it. Who eats all that jam, anyway? Not him. Jam yesterday, jam tomorrow, but never jam today, that's him, I fancy. I suppose it's for the boys. She came back with a great leg of mutton in her basket, so maybe they're coming for Sunday lunch. I don't think Heather has much to say to her mother-in-law, but then that Andrew's a bit of a poor stick. Do him good to get away. Don't you think so?' She spoke to Philip in her mind. But Philip was not there. Since 1947 he had not been there. 'Why?' she begged, 'why?' she demanded, again stretching herself up against the opaque glass of memory, fingers drawn across the coldness, the hardness, to find some new contour that would help her to know. No new bumps, no undiscovered lines, nothing but the familiar, too familiar life, her own story, her version of the lie. Nobody lived now, to help her, nobody knew. 'I am old,' she cried, 'and soon I shall die. Will I never discover why?'

'I love him,' she remembered saying. To her mother, who sat at a high desk, in the old, known sitting-room of the house in which she had first met him. Her mother wore a high-necked blouse, a narrow skirt that showed her ankles as she turned; she was no longer the mother of childhood, turning to soothe and scold a little girl with cut knees, but a woman made to face an alien world that had changed too fast for her. A photograph faced them both from the desk, and it was as if her father were witness to the conversation, adding weight to her mother's words. Fathers, in those days, did not talk to their daughters about such things. It was rare, indeed, that anyone should. One was supposed to sniff it up delicately, like snuff from an ivory box, to breathe it in with the very dust and damask smells of the elegant rooms in which one was reared. There should have been no need to talk; and so her mother let her know, turning to her as she did with such pain, with such dignity, ordering the careful words in her mind before they should dare to touch her lips, for in speaking she denied her upbringing, her beliefs, her whole existence. She herself stood and watched her mother's pain, and it was like a second but a conscious birth. She stood, and waited to be released.

'But, my dear child! You don't know what you're

saying. Really, all this is neither here nor there. You're young, Helena, you must accept my experience for what it is worth. You don't realise what you're doing, you can't realise what this means.'

'But I'm twenty-four. I'm not a child.'

'But in so many ways, you are a child; You have no idea of the risk. You talk like a complete fool, and I can only suppose it's your innocence that makes you do so. Otherwise there is no explanation for this extraordinary behaviour. When I think of the way you were brought up. . . I am baffled, simply baffled, yes and hurt. You are breaking my heart, Helena, I hope you know that.'

'But what do you mean?'

'My dear child, I suppose you know that what you're doing is immoral? That society has a name for people like you? That you calmly talk of living with a man who is not your husband? You can hardly be blind to that fact, even though you seem to be blind to everything else.'

'But he's getting a divorce. As soon as he can.'

'A divorce! And what sort of a recommendation is that supposed to be? This is pure stupidity, the young man is quite unworthy of you in every way, and how you can have gone so far as to compromise yourself in the way you have is beyond my understanding.'

Helena strode backwards and forwards, turning and turning again, to escape. 'I'm not asking you to understand it – or even to condone anything – all I want is to see you again, not to be refused, to be cut off —' She wept, and turned her head away abruptly, because she did not want to be this person, this wrecker who was causing all the pain, and because there was no other way.

'But your father. . .' They both looked involuntarily across at the man who had sat for his portrait long ago in a blackened studio, whose eyes had stared when the camera clicked to preserve his image. 'He'll be back in half an hour, and I don't want him to see you here. It would upset him so much.'

'Don't worry,' she replied, hardened by the knowledge that it was he who must always be protected, whoever else might suffer and die. 'I won't be here. So, it's total war?'

'Oh, how could you? How dare you be flippant at a time like this? Oh, Helena,' there was a sob in her voice, she turned away and dabbed at her face while her daughter stood like stone. 'Darling,' recovering her dignity, 'reconsider, do. There's always a home for you here. If only you'll give this man up. He's no good to you, he's from a totally different background, he's a traitor and he's married. It'd be throwing your life away. It'd bring you nothing but unhappiness and disgrace. No good can come of it, I warn you. But then, of course,' she drew in her lips, 'you must make your own decision.'

'I've made it. I'm going to marry him. You don't seem to understand.' And all the dying gods, society and respectability, safety and propriety, that had paraded before her in that discreet drawing-room, began to retreat, so that she was alone. She had not seen her mother again.

No good can come of it. Other people formed words in their sudden anger that seemed sometimes to hang like thunderclouds over the future. The

70

words became portents. As a girl, standing there in the cool of the room, she shuddered at her mother's words as if from sudden cold, and turned away, determined that this should not be true. Nobody, she said to herself as she left the house and walked in her white shoes out to the dusty drive, nobody has the power to blight one's life, to make careless forecasts like that. It is our own, nobody else knows. And she thought of Philip and knew that she had made her choice in her conscious will; she stood at the bottom of the drive and looked down at the grained patterns of dust upon her shoes, which were new, and looked back at the house where she had spent her life, and then looked away and began to walk, briskly, in the way she had come. And yes, she thought, now, from the other end of her life, there was no false optimism in what I chose; at once, we began to pay. For there had been one night which was blood-red, afire, during which Philip's cool hands stretched towards her through the darkness and were powerless to soothe her, when the child was eventually wrenched from the body that was too thin, too young, she screamed, for all this; and the chaos of the world had invaded her, never entirely to recede. Women she knew chopped off their hair and rolled their sleeves, to labour broad-shouldered in the factory of war. Their lovers were killed, blinded, mutilated, sent home full of gas to mutter forever by the fireside. Philip and she, in their sanity, in their preoccupation with what was, after all, the true centre of life, had escaped. She remembered how he would read out a phrase from the paper and how his intonation, with that touch of mockery, was entirely unlike any other man's

in that year, and how their eyes would meet in perfect understanding across the table, while their quiet
morning bloomed outside. He was sure, he was right;
he looked to the core of things and not to the distract-
ing, scurrying outer rim. And yet this made her
obscurely afraid, looking at him, as his lips shaped
the meaningless phrases and he glanced up at her in
triumph and raised the high arc of his eyebrows upon
the stupidity of the world; she looked and saw him
there, alive, whole, able to say what he felt and do
what he willed, and she smiled back in complicity,
yet was a little superstitiously afraid. There was perhaps always a particular torment left, a personal
ghost that would come out of the corner when one
looked the other way. The world suffered; perhaps
they must suffer too. The hours through which she
struggled to produce that tiny body, the days
through which she dragged her own tired body round
the house afterwards, these must age her. And at the
end of the time, there was the small grave which
might have been her own.

For a time, it was possible to resent him for his
sprightly certainties, possible even to long for their
sorrows to be explicit as other people's were; dealt
out evenly by a government at war – so much for
you, and you, and you – tied in somehow with the
rhythm of things as they were. To be truant was
surely to tempt fate, and fate these days was a surly
monster picking up lives and hurling them away,
twisting love and honour into unrecognisable moulds,
making people end their lives with strange out-of-
character flourishes; men, ordinary people, were like
the faces on hoardings on which somebody had

72

scrawled at random a moustache, a slogan, a hero's laurels; Edward, her silly cousin, died a martyr, so did a thousand others, young men with no particular talent for anything else, while she and Philip, who had decided to live, were called outcasts. The blood had still poured from her for days, she was white and anaemic and moved with a sour lassitude; looking one day at that drawerful of baby clothes she had collected, she thought, how easy to be killed, how nice to receive a sword thrust and die a hero; and how infinitely hard to go on living. But Philip was with her and they clung to each other, braced against the wreckage of this hope of theirs, eye to eye and mouth to mouth in their knowledge that there could be no more children, incapable of looking away. And so they had stayed in their imagination through the years, but the danger was past, the threat gone, the misery old and tarnished. And all the same, she thought, life had gone on.

There had been a walking holiday in Normandy – oh, much later, that must have been. How old was she then, thirty, thirty-five? They stayed in Etretat and climbed down the wooded slopes of hills to a majestic beach. A ragged little boy followed them home one day, all down the shingly beach and home again, until Philip gave him a coin. There were photographs of her on that holiday, showing her standing poised against the white cliffs with her hair in coils, an unbecoming long cardigan stretching almost to her knees over a shapeless skirt, her feet in sensible walking shoes braced on the stones, her face bright as it took up the challenge of Philip behind the camera, smiling her happiness. She had been happy then, the picture was there, somewhere, to prove it. And there was he, more shadowy, wearing some kind of plus-fours and a cap that nearly hid his face. She had photographed him outside their hotel, with somebody's little white dog beside him, and a tree in a pot. So few years later, those bland beaches were ravaged again by attack and carnage, as if one could stand nowhere that would remain quiet. She read about the Normandy landings and the world made 'Normandy' mean something else, not the taste of good food and wine, not the simplicity of holiday, the white cliffs with their mysterious holes, the fisher-men with their berets and their strong brown hands, the steep road back to the hotel; no longer just her husband smiling uncertainly in strong sunlight, be-side a small white dog who could have belonged to anyone at all. Again, there came the public know-ledge to tinge with irony, to distort the private memory. Nothing was small, nothing was private, nothing existed simply to be touched. She felt that she would never go back. 'Extraordinary,' she said now, laying the photograph back in its box, 'to think that was taken before the war. All those years ago. Extraordinary, don't you think?'

Across the fence, lunch was taking place. This was the moment around which the whole day had been constructed, the apex, after which the long Sunday would gradually fall away and disappear; the roast meat and three kinds of vegetable, the apple pie and cream, the cheese and biscuits, these were the offer-ings Felicity had piled upon her altar, a harvest festival of her love. She brought them one by one from the kitchen, her cheeks flushed unusually and her hands nervous, trembling a little in case they might be rejected. In case George might pause, the carving knife lifted from a slice, to ask, 'How long did you cook this for?' as the pink stain on the inner meat condemned her; in case one of the children might not be hungry. But the family ate on imperturbably, leisured in the knowledge that there would always be Sunday lunch, and talked spasmodically, because they were all now at such close quarters. All individual conflicts sank and rocked below the surface; a shallow peace lay across the scene.

'Will you have some more, Lucy?'

'No – no, thank you. I couldn't. It was delicious.'

'Phil?'

'Thanks. Just a little.'

'That's what I like to see. You're getting so thin. Never look after yourselves properly, you children. Andrew?'

'Ta. It's superb, Mum. Congratulations.

She did not smile. Only he said it, while the others did not bother. Only he knew what she wanted, told her what she wanted to hear. She tenderly handed Phil his laden plateful.

'Oh, God, I said only a little. I can't eat this much, Ma.'

'Nonsense, darling, it'll do you good. I know you don't eat properly in that flat of yours.'

'Look, I said I can't eat it.'

'Now, darling, don't. . .'

'Philip, will you keep a civil tongue!'

'Give some to me, Phil,' Andrew said, passing his plate over, 'I could eat a horse.'

'I expect you are!' It was an old, childish, brothers' joke. They fell about, laughing, making faces across Lucy.

'Philip!' George's rebuke came again, harsh with uncertainty.

'Oh, Christ, I was only joking.' He began spiking up bits of potato with his fork.

'There's no need to swear all the time.'

'No, maybe not, but well, I feel the need. Look, can't we talk about something else? Why don't we all pick on Andrew or something?'

'Heather, my dear, I'm sorry, I never asked you if you'd have any more?' Her voice stretched across threatening chaos, bland, with hardly a tremor, so fierce was her control.

'Oh, no thanks, I mustn't. I'm trying to get back to normal. It's awful how fat I got with Jojo.'

'Oh, nonsense, dear, you look fine.'

'I like you fat,' Andrew said. 'How much do you weigh now?'

'Well, I'm back to nine and a half. But I was only just over nine when I started, and then I went up to ten and a half, which was much too much, really.'

'Funny,' said Phil, 'you wouldn't think Jojo weighed a stone and a half, would you? Why don't you call him Jonathan, by the way? Jojo sounds like somebody's dog, and he'll hate you for it when he's older.'

'It's all the placenta and stuff too,' Andrew was saying. 'That weighs. You fool. And all the liquid, too.'

'What liquid?' They rolled each other nearer to the brink, daring her. Once, she could have smacked them, told them to be quiet; now, she did not know; all the borders were blurred, things were funny

76

which had been disgusting, things were serious which had been absurd.

'Now, that's quite enough.' When she spoke, it was as if habit had taken over. 'What a conversation for Sunday lunch. Whatever will Lucy think.'

'Blood or water or something, or perhaps gin,' Andrew said, taking up the challenge, and when she smacked his hand lightly across the table it was because it was all she could do. She did not expect him to take notice. But Philip was away on a different tack, and she turned to him with relief.

'Do you remember,' he was saying to his brother, 'that hide-out we used to have behind the hedge? When we used to leave things out on the path, purses and things, and then twitch them away on the end of a string before the person could pick them up?'

'Yes, and d'you remember the old lady who actually managed to pick something up, and she hung on for grim death and was towed in like a big fish on a line?'

'That was Mrs Fletcher next door, wasn't it?'

'Yes, and she told me all about it at the shops the next day, laughing away in spite of herself. It was a good thing she was so kind about it, I must say. Lots of people would have been furious.' She joined in with them eagerly, and they included her, showing only faint surprise. This was safe ground, the well-trodden past of letter and photograph and reminiscence, where she knew where she was. 'Oh, you were awful, you two. The things you got up to.'

'They were a handful, weren't they?' George was complacently cutting cheese. She breathed deeply with relief.

'And that day you insisted on camping out in the

garden, in spite of the pouring rain? And Andrew coming up to the kitchen door with the rain pouring down his face, asking if we had anything that would kill slugs! Do you remember, George?'

'And those bike rides we went for, after school?'

'Oh, yes, and you remember finding that house, where we thought there was buried treasure?'

'And those terrifying games we used to have in the dark with the kids next door? Really scary. You used to hate it, Mum, everyone crashing around in the dark, breaking things.'

'Yes, didn't I?' she laughed. 'And that time you fell through the greenhouse roof, Phil, do you remember? When I'd told you not to get up there, and you went and fell through on to all those geraniums and came limping into the kitchen pretending you'd fallen downstairs?'

'Yes,' he said, 'and d'you remember when Andrew brought that dog home?'

'Dog? What dog?'

'Surely you remember. The one that had fleas. We hid it in the shed for ages and you couldn't think where all the bits out of the larder were going, and why we kept scratching all the time.'

She said nothing, but George chuckled. 'I can still see you two shifting about from one leg to another, scratching your bites and still trying to make out there was nothing in that shed. I knew you were up to something, all right. You remember that dog business, darling?'

'Oh dear yes. Oh yes, they did go on about having a dog, didn't they? I got quite sick of the whole subject.'

'Oh, yes, we were quite obsessional about it,' Phil said. 'Weren't we, Andrew?' He smiled at her, and she did not know why, but felt the charm work, the evocation of his boyhood turn him towards her again, like a young plant. 'You were naughty, you two,' she said. 'What a dance you led us. I don't know.'

'Oh, I remember,' Andrew said. 'Funny, isn't it, when you look back on things, how petty they seem.' He yawned and looked at his watch.

'D'you think so?' said Phil.

'Oh, and the fuss when it had to go,' Felicity sighed. 'And now, here they are, quite grown up. Doesn't it seem funny?' She smiled at her sons, fortified by the immutable past.

'I remember Andrew crying,' Phil said. 'Do you remember crying, Andrew? About the dog? I remember you crying, night after night.'

Andrew was silent, lighting a cigarette.

'Don't you remember?'

'Oh, well, vaguely. But it all seems so unimportant now, doesn't it?'

'D'you think so?'

'Those bicycles they had,' George was saying, 'I remember teaching them both how to ride them. Every Saturday morning, until they could stay on. And then those long bicycle rides.'

'They used to take picnic lunches.'

'And then they had that stunt of dressing-up as ghosts, didn't they, scaring the vicar out of his wits in the graveyard. My goodness me.'

'Oh, and those awful Guy Fawkes parties, when you used to set off the fireworks for them? Never liked the bangs, did they, when they were little, but then, they soon got used to them.'

'Yes, yes, young Phil used to run a mile when I got out the fire-crackers, didn't you, Phil? Never liked the explosive ones.'

'What happened about the dog?' Suddenly Lucy's clear voice interrupted them. They both turned to her in surprise.

'Oh, we could hardly keep the poor thing. It was covered with fleas and sores and probably had the most awful diseases. Of course, the boys were upset when it went, but then, they soon got over it.'

'We offered to get them another,' George told her, 'but, heaven knows why, it had to be that one or nothing. Such fixed ideas they get. I even went down to the pet shop, but nothing they had there was going to do.'

'Well, but what happened to the dog?' Lucy persisted. Felicity felt herself flush up again, as she did so easily now; she looked at Phil, who appeared composed, at Andrew, who stared at the flowers in the centre of the table and poked the cloth with his fork, at George, who was staring down the table in indignation. Heather alone was turned towards Lucy, relaxed and conversational. 'Yes, what did happen?' she asked.

'Oh, stop going on about that bloody dog!' Andrew exclaimed at last, glaring.

'It had to be put to sleep,' Felicity explained, to put them all at ease and end a conversation that was becoming distressing. 'But of course, one can't expect children to understand that kind of thing. We had a bit of trouble with the boys after it had gone, and it all got rather out of proportion. But of course, it's all such a long time ago, now. Now, who'll have coffee? Heather, my dear, I wonder if you'd give me a hand?'

She stood with Phil and Andrew under the lilac tree, threw the end of her cigarette down in the grass, leaned with a hand upon the rough bark. Heather brought the baby from his pram and laid a tartan rug on the grass, flopped down on it beside the child who was grasping already at grass stems, drawing his fat knees up under him to heave his body across the rug, arms outstretched to seize and explore.

'You sure that grass isn't too damp?' Her father-in-law pounced at once, his brows drawn down to peer at her, head thrust forward like an old man's.

'He's all right on the rug.'

'Well,' he frowned, 'I wouldn't be too sure. Ground gets damp at this time of year, you know. Wouldn't want him to catch a cold.'

'Well, he's only going to stay here while I change his nappy, and then he can go back in his pram. Can't you darling?' Her voice did not change, as she turned from the old man to the baby, but soothed and placated them both.

'Why don't you go upstairs? Wouldn't it be much easier on the bed upstairs?' Felicity Ridgley joined in. Heather looked up at the two of them hovering over her, hovering like something predatory, Lucy thought, but gave no sign of annoyance.

'It won't take me a minute,' she muttered, a safety pin already in her mouth, her hands moving swiftly to wipe the baby's bottom. The little boy kicked his legs wildly, evading recapture. Lucy watched;

Heather, her mouth a little tighter upon the pin, grabbed him by the feet, heaved his bottom in the air to place the clean nappy underneath, and at once a jet rose from his little cock and spouted wet over both nappy and clothes. Like a cherub in a fountain, laughing with pleasure. Heather muttered and the grandparents stood side by side, watching. Lucy saw Felicity's hands move involuntarily, twitching with the information she longed to impose, the help she could hardly resist giving. They were like old vultures, standing there. Lucy moved across the grass, knelt and took the baby's hand. The tiny fingers gripped hers at once, white at the knuckle. The baby tried to get Lucy's finger into his mouth, grinned at her with his wide toothlessness and let out a pleased little shriek, giving her his whole mercurial attention just for a moment, so that Heather could fold and pin the nappy in place.

'Thanks. That seems to have done the trick.' She picked up the baby with a swift gesture, carried him on her shoulder back to the pram and without a word, tucked him in. The baby began to scream at once, in short rasping yells of pure anger.

'Poor little thing,' George leaned over the pram. 'What's the matter? He wants something, Heather. What does he want? Do you think he's hungry? Or maybe his nappy isn't comfortable.'

'More likely wind, I should think,' Felicity said. 'Why not try getting a bit of wind up, Heather? He looked to me as if he might still have a bit of wind.'

'He wants to go on lying on the rug, that's all.' Heather's dark eyes glowered in their pale setting, but her hands were calm, her tone even. Lucy felt an irresponsible urge to rescue her somehow.

'It must be boring for babies, lying in a pram all the time, don't you think?' she suggested; but Heather ignored her, taking silently what she evidently felt to be more criticism. George and Felicity, dissatisfied, moved away, their annoyance written in each line of their bodies. Lucy saw how she would sketch them, how she would draw them cruelly against the grace of the moving trees, shambling in their incompetence. She wandered off alone under the apple trees, her feet scuffing the grass, for the captivity of Heather oppressed her. By her watch, it was only three o'clock, and there were hours before this day could end. She longed for it already, for the disguising darkness, for herself and Phil to be alone somewhere far away, at the house, perhaps, their house with its cleansing sweep of fen, anywhere but here. They would be expected to stay the night. 'What, leave now? I've never heard anything so ridiculous,' Felicity would tell them, her back closing the door. She would be left alone, in a cold chintzy bedroom, without Phil; the window would swing open upon the inscrutable night, and she would be able to lean out and breathe the night air, but inside all would be bright yellow, flower patterns, candlewick, and a narrow turned-down bed. Electricity in all the corners, the walls thin as rice paper. Nobody could ever be so intrepid as to make love in this house, with its thin, listening walls, its lights flashing on at the top of the stairs, its unhappy people lying awake. A cry of joy would go through this house like a sword.

She moved away from them all, down the garden,

which was a long thin one, two wooden fences taper-
ing it nearly to a point right at the bottom, where
there were nettles and a shed. Behind her were
the house, the lawn, clipped by George with a
barber's precision, a belt of indeterminate scrub,
where the mower had not yet reached; and here she
walked through short bristly grass where the apples
lay and rotted, where the hidden toadstools grew and
worms crawled upon twigs, a waste fringed with
little, overworked apple trees with yellow apples
bearing their branches low, and their leaves yellow-
ing too; she had to bend her head ducking the wet
branches as she walked beneath them, so that this
was not so much a stroll as an unnecessary feat, and
her ankles were wet because here the sun had not yet
dried the grass, and there were sharp twigs that
poked between the thongs of her sandals and tripped
her up. Yet Lucy persevered, because behind her
came some spectre of hysteria, so that she had to be,
for a moment at least, alone. The house, as she looked
back at it, mocked her with its deliberate asymmetry.
It had been built at a time when all had to be gnarled
and gnomish, rakish and askew; it was so neatly lop-
sided, so cosily eccentric, as was each of the other
houses in this road, each built to be so individual,
each emerging so exactly the same. This one – and it
could have been in any of them that she had found
Phil's parents – this particular whim of the 1920s had
recently been repainted an acid and lately fashionable
green that lay uneasily against the mottled dark
brown of the timber pinned to the gable and the
purplish colour of the brick. She turned from it,
emerged from under the apple trees and faced a bed

of nettles with a shallow beaten track to the door of the shed. Here George no doubt kept his tools; here he hid from his wife. Here, perhaps, the dog had waited for the sound of boys' voices, the scraps from trouser pockets, stolen from the larder; and they had come, cautiously pushing the door ajar, putting out a hand into the cold and earthy darkness. She pushed up the wooden latch and went in. It smelt of earth and mould, a deep unlit underworld smell, a real potting shed. There were garden tools hanging from nails on one wall, strange grimed instruments, apparently long unused, there was a rickety work bench under the window, cobwebs furled in the corners, on the floor a pile of flower pots, in one corner a mowing machine. A calendar for last year, curled with damp, on the back of the door. She peered out through the dust on the window-pane to make sure that the house, the immaculate lawn, were still there, that she was indeed in the same place, on the same day. There were Andrew and Phil on the lawn, talking, there was the pram under the lilac tree, there was Phil's father, irresolute by the back door, fussing with something; and the house, containing them all, all its rooms tidy. This shed was a corner of someone's mind into which he never strayed, which had never been tidied and made to fit. She pushed open the creaking door that was loose on its hinges and stepped out again into the speckled sunlight of the little orchard. It was then that she looked up, her eye carried all at once beyond the boundaries, over the fence, and saw the face at the window of the house next door. The face of the woman who had waved to Phil that morning and whose wave of recognition had forced them

to go on up the drive and wait for the front door to
open. Then, she had only thought, How nosy. What a
cheek. There was only her own fear and uncertainty,
and the resentment that she had been seen, and now
could not go back; she had not thought further. Now,
she stared back, pushing the heavy locks of hair from
her face that she might see more clearly. The woman,
seeing her stare, did not move away at once on knowing her inquisitiveness observed, but stayed for a full
minute at the window and gazed back at Lucy,
almost as though she gazed through her at something
at her back. Lucy waved, feeling that now some sign
was needed. It was a relief to know that there was
someone else, that she was not the only stranger in a
world of Ridgleys. The woman waved, and Lucy saw
that she had a scrap of white, a handkerchief perhaps,
clutched in her hand, as if she were waving goodbye;
she then withdrew from the window, and the light
curtain swung across it again. Lucy saw in her mind
the figure crossing a room draped with dustsheets,
coming down bare uncarpeted stairs. She stood still
on the edge of the orchard, poised for a moment,
staring at the house next door which now gave back
no sign of life nor habitation, and wondered what it
was like to live there, to peer round a curtain and
watch a girl in pink shirt and blue jeans cross a garden alone, and disappear into a small shed among
nettles. This was such a familiar sensation, this knowledge, sensuously, of what it was to be the other
person. As a child, she had felt it overwhelm her,
when she held an animal, a cat perhaps, clutched to
her and felt that she, Lucy, was the cat feeling herself
held by herself, Lucy, who was the girl. There was

this short-circuiting of feeling, this enclosedness against the outside, this confusion. Yet there had to be a certain distance, a gap of time and space between herself and the woman opposite her, a gap of creaturely difference between herself and the cat. She gazed, felt the recent pressure of palms upon a windowsill and the temptation to return to a window and look out, smelt the dust of enclosed rooms in which all was old, all hers. And moved eventually, shaking her head to free herself, lifting her own hands, to see that they were empty, unmarked, her own. She moved roughly, striding away through the grass, banging a hand in passing against the rough bark of the apple trees – slap, slap – this is me, this is me – slap, slap – I feel, therefore I am – slap – Lucy Kennet, a hundred and thirty-one Lansdowne Road, Lucy Kennet – slap – myself, unique, unique. It was broken, she was free. She ran lightly across the cropped part of the lawn, back to Phil to confront his reassuring otherness, and took his hand, feeling how large, how different it was, swung it in hers gaily between them, glanced up at him so that his mouth moved to ask her what it was and she saw that he was surprised. But the telephone sounded suddenly from inside the house, screamed from all the open windows demanding immediate attention. Lucy jumped. She saw Phil's father, who was nearest to the house, disappear through the back door and block the light in the hall. The scream stopped half-way through, and Phil's mother, who would never be able to let a telephone be answered without her, looked agitated and began to fluster towards the house. She laughed, glad that she was outside it all, balancing on her heels on the grass, like a child, with Phil to hold her hand. In a moment, Phil's father reappeared, looking puzzled and annoyed.

'Philip! It's for you!'

'What?'

'Telephone! It's for you!'

'Who is it?' Phil slowly moved up the lawn, thin as a scarecrow.

'The house, the house,' Lucy said to herself. 'Oh, don't let it be sold. Don't let it all be discussed here. Don't let it be that. But they don't know where we are. They haven't got our number. They wouldn't ring up.'

'Old Mrs Fletcher, lady next door, you know. Says she wants to speak to you.'

Phil followed him into the house. Lucy glanced up at the window of the house next door, asking for an explanation. But the curtains never moved, and no-one came.

'Lucy!' he leaped down the garden, calling her, skidding on soft apples in the grass. 'Where've you been? You disappeared.'

'No, I was here. What was the 'phone call? What did she want? Was it her?'

'Hmm, she wants us to go for a drink this evening. A glass of sherry at six, she said. Sounds frightfully civilised, doesn't it? I used to go round there quite a lot when I was little. Don't know why she suddenly asked us now, though.'

'What's she like?' Lucy asked.

'Oh, old. About eighty, I should think.'

'No, I mean really, what kind of person?'

He considered the question, as if for the first time.

'I suppose, fairly educated, fairly well off, you know. Talkative. Rather odd in some ways. I mean, you often don't know what she's talking about. Kind, though. She's all there, I'd say, only a bit vague. Talks about the past a lot. Her husband died, you know.'

'I thought she looked lonely,' Lucy said.

'What?'

'Just now. I saw her looking out of the window. She waved, and sort of stared out.' She shivered.

'I used to think she was a witch,' he said. 'When I was very small, before I got to know her.'

'There's always someone next door that one thinks is a witch.'

'How funny. Did you?'

'And later on,' she said, 'one's convinced that the person is some kind of crook, and then later on again, one finds out that they're really quite ordinary, just like anybody else. But one never really gets over that feeling of there being someone on the other side of the fence.'

'But you live in a town, in a proper street!'

'It's the same everywhere. There's always something odd, or threatening.'

'Hmm, I felt awful when she caught me one day, creeping round and listening outside windows in case she said any spells. That was the first time I ever went in, and I was dead scared, but she gave me a whole lot of chocolate cake and played records on one of those old His Master's Voice gramophones, you know, with the trumpet, and seventy-eight records, all covered in scratches. She said they were tunes she used to dance to. And d'you know, she even did a bit of dancing round the floor. It was weird. But she's a nice old thing.'

'And he's dead?'

'Who? The husband? Oh, yes, ages ago. Something odd, he had an accident or something. I remember, it was in the papers and Mum wouldn't let me see. Funny, isn't it, how most men die before their wives? I mean, look at all the widows there are.'

Lucy felt the coldness again, that had made her shiver, the fear that had somehow driven her skipping through the grass. 'Well,' she said, 'someone's got to die first, so of course there are widows. I mean, it's obvious. And all the widows – well, most people don't have accidents. And anyway, I wouldn't say there are more widows than widowers. Look at all the feeble old men you see about. Sitting on benches, no teeth, bleary old eyes, nothing in particular to do. Sitting in pubs, shuffling about, getting rheumatism, sucking on a horrible old fag end, drinking meths even, getting put in homes —'

'Lucy!' She knew she was frightening him, she wanted him more afraid than she was, more afraid of the decay, the panic, the aloneness; but he stopped her, putting out his hands, and she took them and they gripped each other as if they saw it changing now, the bright afternoon around them, as if in gripping each other hard they could will away the fear that came coldly round the ankles and picked up the autumn leaves and carried their skeletal forms away to become dust, elsewhere. One turns one's head, she thought, and the moment is gone; one drops somebody's hand and the touch is gone; one stares at memory, and the truth is gone.

90

'You are being ghoulish, darling,' Phil said. 'What's all this in aid of? I may be pushing twenty-two, but I'm hardly in my dotage yet.'

'Who was that?' Felicity asked as soon as he entered. If she had missed a conversation on the telephone, she liked to have it recounted to her all the same. She was in the kitchen, her hand moving evenly to right and left and round in a circle, the spatula smoothing the icing on the cake they would eat for tea.

'Oh, old Mrs Fletcher from next door.'

'What did she want?'

'Asking the children round for a drink, I gathered. Philip and Lucy. Funny, really.'

'She never asks us.'

'Well, we never ask her.'

'But why Philip and Lucy? She doesn't know them. Philip hasn't been round there since he was quite a little boy. Why ask them for a drink suddenly?'

'Perhaps she likes to have young people around her. Cheer her up a bit. You know.'

'I should think that's the last thing they'd do,' she said, out of habit. Phil, with dirty knees, eating chocolate cake; a boy's face that she would not see again, a boy's broad innocent grasping hands. Why did they have to change?

'Funny old thing,' she said, a moment's silence past, her hands poised around the cake. 'Perhaps we ought to do something, I mean, do more about her. She is a neighbour. And old – must be nearly eighty, wouldn't you say? Perhaps we ought to ask her.'

'Well, I don't know,' he said, fingers straying into

the icing to taste, to interfere. She pushed him away in her irritation, and he stood apart, a grown man licking the icing off his fingers. 'There's no point in pushing yourself into people's lives, is there. We've always been good neighbours. We're always there if she wants anything. I've told her that. I've said, if you ever need anything, Mrs Fletcher, be sure to let us know. If she needs a lift anywhere, falls ill, can't manage the tin opener, or wants to use the telephone. And it's not more than a step for her to come.'

'She's got a telephone.'

'Oh, of course, yes. But you know.'

'Hmmm. All the same, it can't be too pleasant, living alone in that house, after that business.'

'What?'

'That business she had over him. Well, it can't feel the same, can it? I don't know how I'd feel.'

He looked shocked. The round eyes, the bushy greying hair, the neck patched with red above the open collar; the broad hands, wedding-ringed, furred; the innocence, the virtue, the dependability. Impossible. She sighed, irritated that he should be shocked. These things after all happened, but not, apparently, to anyone. Foreign blood, funny lungs, fellow didn't fight in the war, that was what George would say; bound to happen, that was what he would say; not surprising and, therefore, not tragic. There was no time for people who messed up their lives by not thinking clearly. There was no effort to accept or understand.

If I were not afraid of him, she thought, I would say all this, just as he stands there, licking his finger and I stand over my cake, I would say it. Phil says it.

I wish Phil would stay, I wish Phil. . . . But there was something uncomfortable about him standing there, just outside her range of vision (unless she turned slightly, and that would be weakness). Her fingers were deft and busy and dared not stop working, and inside there was that familiar feeling, that mounting claustrophobia, making her breath short. The doctor said it could be high blood pressure. She wished he would go away.

'Oh, do go out into the garden, dear. Tea won't be long, I've just got to finish this cake.'

'Tea?' he said. 'But we've only just had lunch.'

'Oh, well, but the children like it. And it is Sunday. I have so little time to sit down, I could do with a cup of tea.'

'If you weren't making tea,' he said, 'you could have been sitting down all afternoon. By the way, have you seen the colour section? I was looking for it all morning.'

'In the downstairs loo. But do go and have a word with the children, they're in the garden.'

'Must've been Andrew. I wondered why on earth I couldn't find it anywhere. I wish they wouldn't take the papers away before I've had a chance to read them. Who pays for them, I'd like to know. Well, what do you want me to talk to them about?'

'Oh,' she sighed at him, 'nothing in particular. Just – well, they're not here for long, I thought you hadn't seen much of them, I thought you might like to go and talk to them, that's all. After all, it isn't as if they came often. Just go and – oh, I don't know – make contact, that's all.'

'Contact? Oh, all right.' There was a man who sat

in the jungle for such a long time, waiting for the gorillas, that eventually after months and months the gorillas came and talked to him, and treated him as one of themselves. She saw him walk uncertainly out into the garden. Four o'clock; she switched off the timer that had been ticking for the cake, straightened the kitchen clock on the mantelpiece. Four o'clock, and she was still in the kitchen, and half the day was gone already. Could a person really ever converse with a gorilla?

3

FACETS of the cold cut-glass struck the light as Philip turned his sherry in his hand, the stem of the glass falling between his fingers. It was cool in the room, where no fire was lit; truly the end of summer. He was saying, 'It seems a very long time since I last saw you, Mrs Fletcher.'

'Oh, my dear boy, it's a long time since you came to this house, certainly. But I've seen you. So many times, coming and going. From school, I suppose, and university, from holidays, here and there, saying hello to your parents, saying goodbye. Oh I've had fun, watching you.' Phil frowned, a small buried convention in him somehow offended.

'You don't mind, I hope? One has to have some amusements, living alone.'

'But you never waved?' Lucy asked.

'Oh, one doesn't want to impose, you know.' She sounded as if she were quoting somebody else. They were silent for a moment.

'But today,' Lucy pursued her thought, 'you waved.'

'Well. Sometimes it feels like time to pluck up one's courage. Things don't always stay the same. Sometimes one just does things, I don't know why. I saw you coming up the drive. . . . Let's just say, today was different.' She was just an old woman smiling at them, encouraging them to talk. 'Is this the first time you've been here? Today must have been quite a change for you, too.'

'We're getting married,' Phil said.

'That's what's new,' Lucy said, 'I've been here before, but you see, it wasn't the same. We've only just decided to get married.'

There seemed to be pain in the old woman's eyes. She frowned and shifted her weight in her chair, as if to ease discomfort. 'Have you told them?'

'My parents? Oh yes. I didn't know how to do it, it all came out at the wrong moment, somehow. I should have been more tactful about it, I suppose. They hate having things sprung on them like that.'

'Yes, I suppose so. It's what happens as one grows old. Surprises, too much change. But were they pleased, really?'

'Oh, I don't know. They think we're too young. Irresponsible. And me being a student, that sort of thing, you know. They think you have to have money

96

to get married, and a job. They can't get used to the idea of students getting married. I suppose it was all so different when they were young.'

'And can you live without money and a job?' she asked, closely. 'Most people can't, you know.'

'We both have grants,' Lucy told her. 'And Phil's twenty-one now and he gets all this money his grand-father left him, in a sort of trust, so we thought we'd buy a house, we found a perfectly beautiful one, not far from here, and we're in the middle of trying to get it.' She felt Philip's stare, but went on. 'Tonight is the crunch. We've got to let the people know tonight, and they'll say if they can accept our offer. It's ter-rible, waiting to know about something.'

Philip said, 'It's all very vague, though, really. Nothing definite, you know. So you won't say any-thing about it, will you?'

'But to whom?' Mrs Fletcher was very bland, turn-ing to him. 'I never see anybody, so you needn't be afraid of that. No, secrets are usually quite safe with me, simply because I don't get tempted to tell them. Anyway, I hope you're successful. Houses are very soothing. But don't forget that houses, property, aren't everything.'

'But a house,' Lucy plunged in, her thin hands in the air, gesturing around a shape. 'A house can mean more than just walls, more than just a place. You know? One makes something, expresses something. And sometimes, one just finds the perfect thing, the perfect place, something that's been sort of waiting for one.'

'And if one falls in love,' said Mrs Fletcher, 'one must act.'

'Yes! That's just what happened! It was as if it had been left there for us, just at the right moment. That's why we have to have it, at whatever risk. Because I do think, don't you . . .' her hands moved again, swiftly, 'that if one is offered something great one is offered a risk too; and if you can accept the risk, you get the greatness. Oh, dear, I am explaining it badly. But no, this is what happens, if you fall in love with a person, isn't it? You risk your whole self, you give yourself away – oh, completely – and it's the most awful risk, but if the person accepts you, then you have the greatness too, oh, and everything.'

'And you can only realise yourself by acting upon the risk,' said Mrs Fletcher, her eyes evading Lucy's to fix themselves upon some mark on the wall opposite, some petal on the potted geranium that was transparent in the sunset, some point in her own mind, or in the past.

'Yes, oh, exactly!'

They talked so rapidly, the words catching fire from each other, the spark leaping backwards and forwards between them, an eagerness and intensity about them as old thoughts fired new ones, fragile thoughts hung like bubbles in the air and a breath alone would keep them there, a movement too harsh would destroy them; Philip sat, leaning forward, his elbows upon his knees, his eyes flickering from one to the other, but he felt excluded. It was uncomfortable to be alone, to be male, to have missed the point; and yet it had perhaps been a point he wanted to miss, for it was frightening to have Lucy give everything so lightly away, both hands stretched out to this old woman, offering the things that were theirs, that were his. He heard her cry out loud, voicing total love, total surrender, he heard her glorify risk and in denouncing caution, somehow denounce him; and a small thought recurred: *Lucy* giving up her*self* to *me*? For was it not Lucy, flashing and lightning-quick, who lit up the rooms they were in, impressed the strangers that they met? Was it not simply to emulate Lucy that he had let fly at his family today, so that she might see how resolutely he was on her side? And after such encounters, which left him drained and trembling, did not her beacon still taunt his darkness, so that compared to her he was large and shapeless and null? To hear her talk of love and understanding merely confused him. He felt it a mistake that he should be there.

'Only,' Mrs Fletcher was saying, 'one risk does not last a lifetime, you know.'

'What do you mean?'

'Well,' the old hand came up to feel the contours of chin and cheek, as if unsure that the flesh it touched would be the old flesh of an hour ago. Mrs Fletcher passed a hand over her mouth. 'One has to go on taking them. Once you've decided on a certain path. You don't get anywhere in one leap. Nothing is conquered in one. I remember my husband saying, Try, try and try again.'

'Oh,' said Lucy, impatient at the worn phrase, 'isn't that just a Victorian idea? You know, if at first you don't succeed? Life being nasty, brutish and short? That kind of thing?'

Phil sighed and passed his tongue over his lips, relieved. The spell, which had seemed to him to hold malice somewhere, was broken. Mrs Fletcher smiled a little sadly and said, 'Well, I suppose I am a Victorian, technically.'

Lucy said, 'Oh, I didn't want to be rude, really, I'm sorry. I just meant something else when I was talking about risks. That after you've taken one great risk, staked your life on it, given yourself up to one great love, there's nothing else you can do. And it's the only way life means anything, to have this private complete commitment, I think. And messing about with jobs and politics and things that you can't really change is just a substitute. It's a way of life I'm talking about, I suppose.'

'So you don't just lie back and rest on your laurels?'

'Oh, no, no, not that. But your decision is made. You're never quite the same again. That's how I feel about this house.' She looked rather primly across at Phil, and smiled at him, telling him that was how she felt about him too. Mrs Fletcher saw the glance and looked across at him too, as if she had only just noticed that he was there. Phil blushed. If only he could believe and belong; there was something shaming about his sitting there, he felt; he was like a man lurking outside a church in the twilight, while a hymn is sung.

'But, my dear, you can't just die at the age of – what are you? Twenty?'

'Nineteen. No, of course not,' Lucy pondered, her brows drawn together in a way Phil remembered from debates at college; she took everything so seriously, she was such a child; and he softened towards her, loving what he called her pomposity, loving the lines on her forehead and her intense blue eyes. But wanting to take her in his arms and tease her a little and kiss her until she laughed, he felt once again helpless, his hands hanging over his knees like useless implements. He frowned, and she looked away quickly. 'But,' she said, 'I wasn't talking about dying. I didn't mean to, anyway. Would it be dying, if one did that? Yes, I suppose you're right.'

It was all nonsense to Phil, she knew, all words and quibbles, unrelated to life. But what Mrs Fletcher said disturbed her. It might be meaningless, but it might be important. Today, it was so hard to sort out what was what. She held out her glass, grateful for the offer of more sherry, the chance to sip and ponder and be unobserved.

Even these two, the old woman was thinking, felt the effectiveness of ritual. Sherry glasses, passed and fingered; the hour of six observed; pigeons flying up somewhere from a wood around a church, while the old clock struck and eyes from all the windows observed them. She looked from the dazed brown eyes of Philip to the intense blue ones of Lucy, where they both sat, rocking their glasses in their hands, twisting their fingers around them, staring into the depths of their little phials of clear liquid, as people did stare into drinks, after all. There was something here that was not yet resolved. She must not make them afraid. But how terrifying, to count each day as a bright bead upon a string, to see each in its entirety and find a challenge in each coming hour; for to her now, time had speeded so that daylight flickered briefly between the enclosing ends of night; one thought took all day, and the simple absence of interruption allowed one to dream from one week's end to the next and notice only casually the passing years. In extreme youth, days were long and an hour's wait painful. Birthdays were important. She saw herself in a schoolroom, reading a book, heard somebody mowing grass outside. The long blade swung its shadow, it rippled across her mind as she read, like a long bird's wing upon a blind. Outside, somebody was sweating above the scythe, his body counting the strokes, as she counted them in the recesses of her mind, way down below what she was reading, way below the feel of the room and the light on the floor and the thin pages turning in her hand. Back and forth the mower mowed, and behind and beyond him stretched the summer, long and broad, empty as the lawn where the grass was cut; and now, one stroke, one movement of that body, one grasp of those hands, tightening upon the worn wood handle, one hiss of the blade through the grass would mean a week, a month, even a year. She was old now, and there must be few strokes left. A blade lifts, a blade falls – she followed the image through the passages of her mind, through the dust and the furniture, the things stacked here and there for no reason – saw the cutting edge in the sunlight, flashing down, the grass flattened, for no reason; saw the blade, rusty now, hooked upon a wall somewhere, a cobwebbed wall, the wall perhaps of an unfrequented shed. A blade cuts, memory lies in tatters, the slashed ribbons of the past; a blade hangs unused, and menace waits where it hangs, and one is given no reason. She shuddered, feeling the room suddenly cold, and stretched out a hand to feel the warmth of the fire, forgetting that there was no one now to light it if she did not.

'Tell me about your house,' she said, for that was where their thoughts were. Lucy heard Phil begin to speak.

A blade hangs unused, and there is menace. She had marched up to that front door, her red hair flying, her face set against adversity, she had walked with Philip, arm in arm, and they had both been young warriors, scorning all around them, stiffening their limbs for the coming fray; and had paused, a minute, on the threshold, and seen Mrs Fletcher pull back the curtain and tap fragile fingers against the glass, and had felt, at that moment, impelled to go on. And after that, what could they have done? After that, Lucy thought, did one cease to be oneself and become what another imagined one to be? I am Lucy Kennet, Lucy Kennet, slap, slap, slap, slap; the bark of the tree is hurting my hand, therefore I exist. But to Mrs Fletcher, what had she been? I am only nineteen, she wanted to shout, I am only young, I cannot be all these things, I never knew your world, I live in my world, my dream, my house, and I do not understand. I am only myself. But, herself? How very little, after all, was left; she was whittled down, shaved to a white stick, an ash twig floating on the wind, never to come to rest. The words tinkled like the notes of a tinny piano upon the surface of her mind, but the images behind them left an imprint like a footstep in earth; she listened, and saw herself in a white dress, seated at a piano, and Philip leaning over her; she saw tall grass in summer, and men coming down to mow; she was in the dark, something familiar, something recent, and there was light outside, green, filtered, remote, and there was the smell of earth.

But she cried, this is not me, this is something I know nothing about, you can't pin it on me, you can't make me suffer these things. And she pleaded, I am only nineteen, I am only nineteen.

'It's a large, squarish sort of house, built in yellowish bricks, with a greyish roof, and some of the floors are stone,' Phil was saying.

'The bricks aren't yellow,' she interrupted, 'they're more a sort of pinky-brown. And the roof isn't really grey, it's red, I'm sure.'

'It's grey! Honestly, Lucy, you never notice anything, do you?' He turned to Mrs Fletcher, 'I don't think she knows what anything looks like, it's quite extraordinary. I don't think she'd ever be able to find her way home on her own, she'd simply wander about looking for landmarks which don't exist.' He laughed, apologising for her.

'Well —' she felt her anger rise, as if he had taken some unfair advantage, 'Well. It's in the middle of nowhere, anyway, very quiet, with flat land all around it, like Holland. And there's one tree by the gate. And you can see for miles, dykes and fields and little stunted trees and black earth, full of potatoes. Or was it celery? Anyway, very good earth. It feels like the middle of Russia. You know, you could imagine that flat countryside stretched on and on forever, in all directions, and every now and then there's a village, sort of huddling together, with its back to the wind. Huge amounts of sky. It's the least claustrophobic place I've ever seen.'

'You can't mean it's like Holland *and* Russia,' Phil said. 'You must mean one or the other.'

'How do you know they aren't alike?' They had

104

stood in the lane outside the house with their backs to the house and the tree, facing out across the fen, and he had said 'This must be what Holland's like. Did you know that the man who drained it all was a Dutchman?' informing her, as he always did, as an after-thought and without emphasis. And she had said 'It gives me a feeling of what the middle of Russia must be like. Land going on forever, until you get to some frozen port.' And he had agreed, un-critically, and taken her hand for a moment while they stood in silence, just looking, this land, as she thought, their Kalamazoo or Kazakhstan, it did not matter which; it was empty, black, wide open, to be filled with their dreams and made into their country.

'I expect they might be alike,' Mrs Fletcher said. 'Flat, anyway. And flatness gives a peculiar perspective to the rest of life, don't you agree?' They agreed, bowing their heads to her calmness, but Lucy was stung with a sense of failure.

'It's got great big rooms with low ceilings upstairs, anyway,' she plunged in again, calling up words to help her. 'And from the bedroom window there's this amazing view, which you could see when you lay in bed. And you'd always hear the wind, and the twigs tapping against each other, but underneath the sounds, this incredible silence.'

'Mightn't it be rather lonely, right out there?' the old woman asked mildly, for now she had nursed them back to some sort of equilibrium, she could continue her challenge. 'Or do you like the country that much?'

'Well, neither of us has ever really lived in the country before. So it'd be a sort of challenge. A risk,

105

as you said. We felt we wanted to get away from –
oh – all this —' her arm gestured, taking in the room,
the house, the street, in one movement. 'We wanted
to start something on our own. To be free of it all.
Oh, I don't know, it may sound mad, but the world's
so awful at the moment, all war and diseases and the
ghastliness in towns. Did you know they'd cut the
tops off all those trees on the road into town? We
came past on the bus, it was simply appalling. That
sort of thing. And getting up at seven every morning
and trekking off to work, and coming back just in
time to slump in front of the telly and then trudge off
to bed. We just thought we wouldn't accept that sort
of life. And all the awful implications, the bureau-
cracy, the oppression. Do you think it's awfully
escapist?' She looked at Mrs Fletcher anxiously, and
Phil again felt a tremor of misgiving. Their lives, their
futures were to be fashioned in this room, it seemed;
the bright dark eyes of Mrs Fletcher were scanning
their intentions, while they waited for approval. She
was spreading her hands on her knees, looking down
at the rings, the wrinkles, the folds of pale and
mottled skin. 'Quite often, people say things are
escapist because they don't dare to do them themselves.'

'Oh, do you think so?' broke in Lucy.

'Yes, but at other times, one is escaping because
one does not dare. The world has always been uncomfortable, sad, full of wars. In our generation, we
tried to escape from them too, my husband and I.
But who is to say who is right?'

'My father fought in the second war,' Phil said, and
then wondered why he had said it.

'Oh, did he?'

'What I mean is, I think he's – they're – jealous, my parents I mean. Because they didn't have any chance to move out.'

'Yes, I know what you mean,' said the old woman, feeling her age, her heavy and wrinkled hands, her used, tired body and her wandering mind, more acutely now than she had for some time past. 'But still, everybody has some kind of choice.' Phil thought she looked now like a very old reptile. She saw him look at her, and saw him turn away. 'Don't they?' she insisted.

Felicity Ridgley stood alone in her kitchen, poised above her own tidiness for the second time that day, and felt time hang in the air, not moving, about her. Her mind was like a hawk in the blue, aimless, hovering, jerked only now and then out of lethargy by the sudden drive to pounce. She pounced upon crumbs, lost buttons and stray hairs, her fingers hurrying to sweep, dust and tidy; she pounced upon a thought, a suspicion, and clawed it up, clutching it to herself as if she feared to drop it, and carried it with her up to her domain in the air. Now, she stared at the kitchen table, her eyes vague but her fingers clenched together belying the vagueness. There was time between tea and supper. There was time to do something, make something, tidy something away, time to summon the scattered remnants of the day and bend them to her will. The children were out of the way; this of old was a comforting thought, for it brought an image of them both tucked up, asleep, in their neat white beds after a goodnight kiss; and she would not be bothered for an hour or so. Where were they really? Andrew was upstairs with his wife, helping her put the baby to bed – too kind, too useful, Andrew was to that girl. She did not know what adversity was. And fancy making Andrew change the child's nappy in the night. For Heather, she wanted hardship. Some cruel challenge, even, something to wipe away that smooth veneer, cripple that calm optimism. It irked her to see her happy and careless with her son. Yes, there was the shout from the bathroom that told of the three of them playing together, as if the parents too were children. It was not right, somehow, that they should have no proper idea of the seriousness of life. It was shocking that they should have a child and not know. And as for Philip, as for Philip and Lucy, out of the house for a blessed hour or so, she thought – what was one to do about them? There was a new hardness in Philip, that made one shrink from him. Just let them walk back in here, into this kitchen, cool as cucumbers, expecting dinner; just let them take her for granted, just let them treat the house like a hotel and think nothing of their rudeness, just let them, and they'd soon see what they had coming to them. She would not put up with it; she was not going to let herself be used like that, like a cook, like a housekeeper, or a scullery maid; and in her own house, too; and his own mother, who had sacrificed so much. She stood so, poised over the kitchen table, her fingers clenched upon one of the fragile green-handled little knives they had used at tea; and her eyes were fixed on a far object, something in the garden, something for which the growing darkness and the uncurtained glass were pierced by her gaze, but which nobody, coming at that instant into the bright and lighted kitchen, would have been able to see.

Phil said, 'But how can one have a choice, really? Everything's there before you're born. All the things other generations have done, in their turn, I suppose, without a choice. And they go on after one's dead. You can't change anything. You can only decide not to accept it. You just have to go and do your own thing, as they say, and let the rest get stuffed, if they want to. It's too late. One doesn't have time.'

'Just one life,' Mrs Fletcher said, not answering him, her eyes blurred now with fatigue. 'Just a few years. You make choices all the time, of a sort. But who's to tell you if you were right?'

It was Lucy's turn now to look from one to the other and to feel the words weave a net around her, incomprehensible, threatening. She could not see what either was saying. What was choice, what the absence of choice? Her glass was empty, and she wanted to go. It was a pity they had left their cigarettes behind; for to light one now, to lean back and blow out smoke would change things and make her the one in control. She felt herself in another life, long-legged, urbane, blowing out smoke; but they had left them behind. She leaned forward instead, hands clasped around her knees, tension in the muscles of her back. They had been sitting here such a long time; she was tired and wanted to go.

Phil said, 'Well, I suppose we ought to be going, really,' but yet did not move. She sat tense, looking at him, willing him to move and stretch, so that she could stand up and they could move gradually, as couples did, towards the door. That was it, she thought, that was what life will be like. I shall always be waiting for him to move.

Felicity picked up a newspaper, to fold it and shut it away with others in a kitchen drawer; she tried not to see it, but as usual it was no good. He was there still, the man in the cell. She picked newspapers daily off the drawing-room floor, off the breakfast table when George had been reading them. Your eye was caught by headlines as a fish is impaled on a hook; and as it struggles free, even, it is bogged down to flounder in the small print. She could not put it down, not yet, but stood there as if compelled, the folded square in her hand, reading. Surely, she told herself, it was never like this in the war, surely I never, surely . . . but what she told herself faded, as if some-one had turned down the sound, and she was drawn into direct contemplation again of the man in the cell. He had different faces, he was of different nationalities; and yet she knew him. They invented terrible things to do to him, and the details were there, explicit, so that one knew that anything they had left out must be worse than that, worse than the worst, more unimaginable than the unimaginable, and yet fully accessible to her own imagination. She saw his dark, lined face, was aware of bloodstained cloths, ropes, wires, the smell of damp, the grit upon the floor; and she had promised herself, oh, so many times, that she would not be caught, that she would not allow herself to think of him again, not look at a newspaper, in case, not switch on the television unless George were in the room, who could not stand anything 'morbid' and would switch off after the weather forecast; but it was no good, it seemed; his cries were in the very air, his eyes met hers in the sunlight as in the dark, a whispered, innocent word was enough to conjure him up, to make her tremble and sweat and want to cry, so that people would think she was going mad. Nobody else she knew cried in the street, passed newspaper sellers with eyes averted. Nobody else, apparently, was personally and remorselessly haunted. It was months now since she had heard of his capture; and during those months he had worn a dozen different faces, cried out in different languages, been accused of different crimes; but it was always to her that he had appealed. And they had tied him up and beaten him on the soles of the feet, and done a hundred other unmentionable, inconceivable things; and because there was no charge, no crime of which he stood accused, there was similarly no excuse, no absolution for her. She thought of pain rushing up through the body, harassing the mind; and wondered if she could stand it all much longer. She wanted to write to him, send him parcels, tell him that she cared. But of course, they had guards, censors. The gap was impossibly wide. So at night, when the certainties of her childhood returned to her, when George had finished reading his book and had switched off his bedside light, heaving a broad shoulder towards her with the bedclothes stretched tight over it, she prayed for him. It was hardly prayer, perhaps, in that prayer meant some kind of communication; she called it to herself 'concentration'; and nightly she forced herself to think of him, to concentrate on him as in the previous few minutes she had concentrated on Phil, Andrew, George and the Queen, to dwell on his face and his predicament, to absorb all the facts of his pain and his helplessness, and perhaps commend him to a person who might exist, an almighty who might miraculously combine knowledge with lack of cynicism, power with mercy. Without George knowing, for she would have been confused if she had to explain, she lay on her side nightly and with silent lips framed his unpronounceable name, in the syllables of a language which she could not speak; and slept, a little comforted.

'Yes, we really must be going,' Phil said, and got to his feet. 'It must be nearly supper time, isn't it? Ma can't stand it if we're late. I don't know, I wish she'd find something else to think about besides endless meals.'

That dog; for an unwelcome moment she let her mind dwell upon that dog. That, she had told her husband, had been the beginning of the rot. The thin end of the wedge. There was always a point at which people began to take advantage of one. Even people one loved, people one had created, began to impinge, to take things, to take advantage. She felt, over that dog, some obscure conspiracy of dirt and chaos; the thought was repellent that it had been there, in that shed at the bottom of the garden, with its fleas and its straggly, smelly hair, for days at least, while she had been unaware of its existence. It frightened her as disease frightened, it was deadly as a lethal germ.

The sight of her small sons snivelling when she found out filled her with anger. They stood in front of her, nine and six years old, already wanting something which she could not provide, already in arms against her.

'But he hasn't got a home,' Andrew said, standing a little in front of his brother, the spokesman.

'Well, it can't stay here.'

'But, Mum . . .' it was the whining, wheedling tone she remembered so well. Phil, she remembered, had simply stood there with tears in his eyes about to overflow, and she had wanted to take him in her arms and comfort him, but was irritated afresh by her own pity.

'But, Mum, why can't he stay? We'll look after him, won't we, Phil? We'll buy his food, and we won't let him make a mess, honestly.' They stood there in their sleeveless Fair Isle jerseys, their grey shorts and shirts; their shorts hung over their knees; they were somehow pathetic, with their shorn heads and their thinness. Somewhere, she was aware of what they were feeling – there had been something, was it an animal, an unsuitable friend? – but no, she knew what to do, she knew, after all, what was best.

'A dog like that can't help making a mess. It's bound to have fleas, and look at that raw patch in its ear. No, I'm afraid it'll just have to go.'

Phil spoke, she remembered, for the first time. 'I don't know why you have to call him 'it' all the time. He's a he, and his name's George.'

'George? But that's. . .' It was their father's name. It sounded strange on a child's lips.

'I know it's Daddy's name,' said Andrew. 'But it doesn't matter, does it?'

'This is a different George,' said Phil.

It had all been most unpleasant, getting the animal into the back of the shooting-brake and taking it off to the vet's. It was a dreadful dog, spineless somehow, broken down perhaps by a life of starvation and homelessness. Heaven knows where they had found it. It had runny brown eyes and a tail that quivered between its legs, a tail like an old feather, thin and sparse. It was large and heavy and inert. It lay in George's arms without moving, as he put his arms around its chest and half-dragged, half-carried it to the car. George dumped it quickly on the sacking in the back, shaking his sleeves and coat tails in the air, in case of fleas. He kept on saying, 'Of course, this is far the best thing for him. Don't you worry, darling.' Telling her not to worry, as if she cared. She wanted to shout out, 'Go and tell that to your precious sons, then!' and then to put on her coat and walk quickly right away from the whole scene. Instead, she got into the shooting-brake beside him and stared straight ahead of her in silence, while he drove. The dog sat in the back and quivered. She fancied that she could feel its eyes upon the backs of their necks. The boys had been at school at the time. Afterwards, neither of them had spoken of it again.

'When's supper, dear?' he was in the kitchen now, George with his slow Sunday afternoon air, wondering what to do.

'Usual time.'

'Oh, yes. Oh, I see. Well, I think I'll just go for a

114

little stroll. Look, why don't you have a rest? You've been at it all day, slaving away in here. Why don't you go and put your feet up for a bit? Read the papers. Give yourself a break.' She had thought for a moment that he was going to ask her to join him on the little stroll. It was so long – years perhaps – since they had sat together at the bar of the local pub, she sipping a ginger beer shandy, he with his pint; and even then, there had not been much to say.

'Oh, how can I?' she replied, tired rather than angry, tired of the old refrain, tired of her own fear and reticence. It was so much easier and more comfortable to stay where one was. 'With all these people to feed? It's no picnic, you know, when there are six people sitting down to every meal.'

He simply sighed, and said, 'You let them make a doormat out of you. Why you don't get some of those young people in to help, I don't know. But then, you will do it all yourself. You will go on and flog yourself to death, providing meals for them all. Do them good to fend for themselves, for once.' It was more than he had said for a long time, though, and he was standing there actually looking at her, actually looking as if he saw her, in her apron with her hair all messed, just as she saw him suddenly, his blue eyes, grown watery, that had been so hard, like blue stones, when he was young. His red face and his sloping shoulders, the grey hair like stubble. 'Why not come out with me for a bit? Just a little stroll. We might go down to the Eagle, if you like, have a pint before supper. It must be nearly opening time.'

She put out a hand, to stop him, for there was no response to this, there was no refuge. Once she had lain face downwards on a hotel bed, and he had come and caressed her round bottom through the sheets, his hand burning and heavy as lead, and he had said 'You've a lovely rump, Felicity,' and had tried to make her come out and be seen, naked as she was, by him who sat there fully dressed, in the cruel white glare of morning. She clutched the sheets around her and lay cocooned, hoping that if she lay stiff enough, his hand would go away. For how could one know that one would not be mocked?

'No,' she said, pleading with him. 'No, I can't. Please don't make me. I'd rather stay here.' I'd rather stay, limbs tight to my sides, sheets cleanly wrapping me, like a mummy, like a corpse; eyes closed, face turned downward to the kind pillow, shutting out the morning light and those peering, opaque eyes. But how nice it would be, just this once, as it was, after all, her birthday, to be able to say, 'Yes'. Casually, 'Yes, all right, dear.' That'd be nice. It might be different, they might start again . . . any day, any day, she told herself, can be the one that changes things, you're never too old, it's never too late; one day, you just say casually, 'Yes, all right', and everything works out. But not today, not yet, not yet.

'For God's sake, Felicity,' he was saying, his voice hard, 'I only asked you to step down to the pub with me. I don't know what the hell's the matter with you, these days. If you ask me, you'd better see a doctor. Dr Miller'd give you something. Go and see him on Monday, for God's sake. Now, are you coming?'

'No,' she faltered, 'no, George, I can't. You see —' But he had already left the room.

*

Yes, that business with the dog had driven something underground. It was as if they had buried it in the garden, and had to step daily past its grave, eyes averted. Philip had become deceitful, it had even been written, to her shame, on one of his school reports. She saw him as a small boy, setting off to have tea with Mrs Fletcher, standing before her as she licked the corner of her handkerchief and rubbed a smear from his cheek, before he went; he had his hair smarmed down in imitation of Andrew, and his school jacket was buttoned up rather tight over a non-uniform jersey. He had promised to eat politely and not to forget to say thank you. His grey socks pulled up tight to the knee, he had strode off down the drive, never once looking back. Felicity saw him hook the iron hook over the gatepost and turn to walk up Mrs Fletcher's drive, ring the doorbell, stand a moment still and stern upon the step, greet Mrs Fletcher gravely when the door was opened, walk in and shut the door behind him. It was only later that she discovered that he was in the habit of nipping in to see Mrs Fletcher at all hours, to drink coffee with her, perch on her stool in the kitchen while she cooked and tidied, watch her gardening and carry her heavy wooden basket full of weeds; only later that she realised that the departure to afternoon tea had been a carefully staged performance for her alone. She began to watch him, to track him. She slapped his hands at table when he reached out for the jam, demanded to know what he was reading, held herself back from him when he cried; and all the time, there was a part of her that was sad, while the other part said things like 'It's all for his own good' and 'He's got to learn'. Because she loved him, somebody had decreed, they must both suffer. He, meanwhile, looked at her sideways over his uneaten food and was dumb to her questions, resisting with all the strength of his six or seven years the force of her inquiry. The long duel between them had begun. This evening, going gladly off with Lucy, to drink sherry with Mrs Fletcher, his glance told her that there was nothing she could offer him which they, the young woman and the old woman, could not. This afternoon, as he flashed his defiance in the hall, his eyes lit hers with a brief caress, before the wound came, telling her plainly, 'Because I love you, we must both suffer.' And she, as he as a child had done, stood mute under the sentence.

Now she drew the curtains of the kitchen with a fierce movement against the darkness, as if at once she pulled shut a curtain in her mind; turned her eyes inward, to her house, to her home. How many people were there really for supper? Would there be enough of that soup she had made yesterday, and would potatoes in their jackets and salad be enough to go with the ham, or should she do some hot vegetables as well? Her arms spread wide across the table, she cleared it of unwanted clutter. With the curtains drawn, the house was safe from prying eyes and tapping branches, from the whole, complex, terrifying, dark outside. She touched the scrubbed surface of the table with pleasure; it was clean and it was solid. She glanced towards the pots of spices and herbs that sat in a row upon a shelf, dusted daily while the herbs grew old and tasteless within, and was reassured to see that they were all still there.

118

Pepper, tarragon, turmeric, sage; rosemary, parsley, basil and thyme; pepper, tarragon, turmeric – George did not like his food spiced, so they were rarely used and she hardly knew their tastes, but their names were strong magic and would serve her to the end.

4

'LUCY, Lucy.' He spoke fiercely against her mouth, into her hair, hands reaching to fill themselves with her flesh, grip her to him, twist from her the cry that she needed him as he needed her, that she was his. Red hair, golden hair, soft skin softly tanned, summer's marks leaving her breasts and buttocks white as ever, shadow to be hunted in the hollows of knees and hands, grass in the smell of them together, heat and dryness, the long cool of rivers, warm porridge oats on the breath afterwards; images chased each other, falling down before the reality, the touch, the taste he wanted. It was no good standing here like this necking in the hall.

'Oh, Phil. Oh, what are we going to do? We must find somewhere somehow.'

'Do you love me, do you want me, do you want me to fuck and fuck and fuck you, and fuck you, and fuck you —' he had to say it, he whispered it fierce as ever into her ear, the words hurting him a little with each blow that fell upon a taut wire; he had to know, to hear her, to feel her with him and know that she was there, because otherwise reality fell away, and all was watery and soundless as a dream.

'Yes, yes, of course. Oh, sod being here, sod your parents, Phil, and this bloody house. Look, there must be an attic, a room where nobody goes —?'

'No unknown corners in this house, Lucy. This house is all above board and out in the open. They knew what they were doing all right, building houses like this. There's only the garden – and the shed.'

'I don't much like the shed.'

'Ni moi non plus. Merde, alors. Oh, Lucy.'

'What about your bedroom. Surely there's a lock on the door?'

'Well, yes, I suppose there is. But it'll be supper time soon. I mean, they'll be wondering where we are.'

'Let them wonder,' she said, and was surprised at the anger in her own voice. She was pulling him to her again, in the half dark where the coats were hung, a narrow corner of the hall that smelt of wellingtons and tweed; pressing him against her, for she could feel his will ebb, in spite of his hot body, and there was disappointment and remorse in that fatally receding tide. Her hands passed again and again over the smooth skin beneath his jersey, her

122

fingers rode down the shallow ridge at the base of his spine, and went back and forth, deeper and deeper, until they wedged in the tightness of his trousers and could explore no further than the hillocks that clenched like fists beneath them. Naked, he was like a dry brown leaf after the summer's sun, and he had black hair like a cap, and growing mysteriously in tufts, softer and darker still, hidden now beneath his clothes. Skinny, she called him, skin-and-bones; but her lips could play between his ribs, her head lie held in the hollow of his stomach when he lay flat; and his knees were the graceful knees of young cantering horses, his lifted chin that of a young horse scenting danger; his long back the curve of a wave in brown water.

'Oh, come on,' she begged. 'Let's go upstairs. I can't bear it. This is worse than the three-and-nines.'

'Don't know where you go for three-and-nines these days,' he muttered, his hands resting for a minute flat against her shoulder-blades, under her shirt.

'There's nothing wrong, is there?'

'No, no. Oh, Lucy —'

'Come on, then,' she said, 'I love you.'

They went silently up the stairs with downward glances, but nobody came; and along the landing was Phil's bedroom, where he had slept as a boy. A narrow bed, yellow-counterpaned; his ties and shoes strewn about; the smell of a long absence.

'*Swallows and Amazons*,' Lucy said, reading along the line of titles on the mantelpiece, '*Eagle Annual*?'

'Oh, Ma would keep them, for some reason.

Sentimental, I suppose. Still, you never know, they might be good post-coital reading.'

'I suppose they might.'

'Lucy?'

'Yes?' She sat beside him on the bed and looked sideways at him, afraid of what indecision she might see. He felt a firm hand unzip his trousers, a warm hand burrowing like a mole. She was looking up at him now, her bright eyes pleading, and her hair hung like copper wire where he had tangled it, he saw her breasts rest gently in the white cups of her bra, down the gap where he had pulled away her shirt. His hands went down the gap, groping, to reassure, to stroke and knead, his fingers seeking out her nipples, his lips on her throat again while she was spread beneath him like a white plain, a land he had crossed in dream, his familiar country and she cried out 'Phil! Phil!' in her frantic haste, scrabbling at the tight trousers he wore, so that he had to stop and laugh and remove them himself; and she lay there secure in the knowledge that in moments, in seconds they would be there, and remarked that in the old days, it had always been the man who had trouble undressing the lady in question. But as she laughed, he was upon her, hot and hurried as a schoolboy, and in one noisy, clumsy, clashing second it was all over, he cried out and was gone, and she was alone somewhere out on a rocking sea, stranded beneath a pitiless sun. There was a bald bulb in the light overhead, that swung to and fro, the sprigged curtains rippled against the window, the childhood books stood ranged and neat, the dark head of her lover lay soaked upon her chest, and along the passage, with

124

little clicking steps, someone was coming. Beyond the light curtains, behind the closed panes, it was already quite dark.

Mrs Fletcher thought, pulling her upstairs curtains against the chill September night, how early it gets dark these days, soon it will be quite dark by tea-time, and the afternoon will be only a glimmer of grey, making it not worth while to go out, or indeed to do anything. These autumn nights, for all their bonfires of sunsets and their seas of stars, made her long always for the twilight nights of summer, through which one sat and played patience, or talked, or just thought, but which made no demands, so long, so gentle they were, upon one's time. There was time for everything, in summer; but these shortening days made one hurry, so that each action was simply a preparation for the next and nothing was true simply to itself; one drew curtains in order to make up fires, so that one might eat in front of them, and then go to bed; one woke in the morning, and thought immediately of the afternoon. Everything hustled one along, reminding always that the true meaning of winter was sleep; and only going to bed had any finality. One rediscovered one's affinity with moles and tortoises and all creeping, tunnelling, sleeping creatures. She thought of lying with her paws over her eyes, wrapped in dead leaves in the hollow of a tree, never wondering whether it was this winter which would bring death; for death would be simply a part of sleep. To be awake, to get up and dress and boil eggs and potter in the kitchen before dawn was to lay oneself open to the shock – the ring of the doorbell, the tap on the blind – that told one life was over. She would be standing in the kitchen, perhaps, with a spoon in her hand, with an egg in it, the egg drying quickly in patches, boiled and ready to eat; the steam would rise in her face from the swirling inside of the pan, she would be there, present, conscious in the midst of her consciously ordered life, and the knock would come, there would be a step in the hall, the spoon would shake and the egg fall from it, to scatter in a wet mess of white and shell that she would never see, for between the spoon and the floor, in that brief drop, it would have happened. I am not afraid, she said, except of that moment – the moment after one hears the burglar, the moment before one knows it is only a cat. She said, one is never old enough.

She crossed the landing, drawing the stair curtains firmly together. It had been a good buy, that green velvety stuff they had bought before the war in D. H. Evans; it had made curtains for their house in Oxford, and then for the hall and stair windows here. She had sat, with the green stuff flowing all across her knees for days, pedalling away at an old sewing-machine, peering in the poor light. It must have been winter. Phil sitting opposite her, reading a paper, his chin hidden in his hand. She went downstairs slowly, her hand lingering on the polished banister rail, straightening a picture on the wall, the print of Hampton Court that someone had given them, sometime. Hampton Court. Green lawns and banks of heliotrope, lion and unicorn rearing against the sky, herself and Phil standing under an archway and talking about Sir Christopher Wren. She passed on down the stairs. The stair carpet was covered with fluff and needed hoovering; but even with that new Hoover dustette thing, it was an effort to get it out and bend one's knees and poke about after the dust. What was dust? What was being old, if one could not live with a little dust? Lucy had run upstairs during the evening to go to the lavatory, and she was sure that Lucy had not noticed the dust. Letting oneself go, that was the phrase one heard so much of, these days. All that stuff about the most glamorous grandmother, all those blue rinses and wrinkle removers. If she had bothered with all that, she would have been a goner long ago. She paused at the bottom of the stairs and looked in the hall mirror, a thing she did not often do, now. But her small vanity was still justifiable, the face she saw was handsome still and seemed to carry within it the fey beauty she knew had been hers. A witch, a fairy, Philip had called her, teasing her for her pointed ears. Unfashionable to look at, she had been then; then, it was all the statuesque and the Grecian that one aimed at. Bosoms and plump arms. But of course, all that went out after the war. That was the face, though, that was the face. . . . She stepped back, pleased with her memories. A cousin, kissing her in the nursery doorway – they could not have been more than fifteen – and a boy in a Midshipman's uniform, at a party. 'You're awfully pretty,' he had said, his brass buttons winking, and had gone off, having filled her programme, to find her an ice. And somebody at Oxford had written her a poem, something about fire, 'Fire goddess, fairy of the fire', something like that, because of her reddish, golden hair. Lucy Kennet's hair.

Mrs Fletcher felt moved at this point to go into the sitting-room and pick up the portrait of Philip that stood just inside her desk, beside the crisp piles of writing paper and envelopes that were so seldom used. She stared down at him, willing the face to tell her more, scrutinising the tender mouth and the large dark brimming eyes, the little dark moustache with the lip underneath that she had never seen naked, the broad brow and the slightly receding chin. The eyes in the photograph were black pools, each holding a fleck of light. She gazed at these flecks until her eyes hurt her. Her hands shook, she saw the edge of the photograph quiver against the curtain, grazing the cloth, disturbing minutely the hanging folds. She sighed, and put it back on the desk. There was something that would never be known, seek how she might. The scythe swung remorselessly, its shadow clearing the sunny yellow curtain, blocking for a second the beam of the summer sun, casting its own steel chill like a small cloud that shivers over the earth on a blue, baking day in July; it had been raised and had fallen, and now it was too late; the hour, the moment at which she could have known was sliced off forever, it lay untouched like a shaving upon a dark floor, somewhere where the door was shut.

The clock in the hall struck seven. The house was so empty, she heard it creak around her, and shivered a little, for the gas fire in the sitting-room gave only a feeble heat and its transparent straight flame little comfort. Usually, the house was simply her shell; usually it fitted her as comfortably as did her clothes. But tonight it missed perhaps the careless, cheerful company of Lucy and young Phil. It seemed full of corners, and pointless areas of space. As she moved about it, gradually doing all the little things that led eventually to going to bed, there were great stretches of wasteland to be crossed, it took a long time to get from one place to another, her steps needed to lengthen into strides as she moved from stair to hall to kitchen; and objects which used to be in easy reach now seemed high and inaccessible, as if they taunted her. She felt very tired. She leaned for a moment against a wall and heard her heart beat. People said sometimes, when a husband had died or children left home, that they rattled in their houses. Dead peas in a dried-out pod. She had not felt that she rattled in hers, not even when Philip was dead, not even when for the first time in her life she had found herself alone. Then the house had shrunk kindly to accommodate her and to soften her loss. She had always been able to live in all the rooms and know what they were for. There were no corners that she dreaded, nor cupboards she avoided looking into, nor rooms in which she felt uncomfortable and upon which she quickly shut the door. That way, she had always felt – the way of old women who peered under beds and behind doors – that was the way of madness. A friend had told her once that she looked under the bed every night to make sure that Dr Crippen was not there. The friend had rolled an orange under the bed, she said, and if the orange came rolling predictably out on the other side, she knew it was all right. But imagine, Mrs Fletcher thought, imagine the orange not coming out. Imagine lying in bed, dreaming of a madman underneath you, eating oranges; or worse, imagine Crippen catching the orange as it rolled, giving a silent little chuckle under his horrid moustache, and casually spinning the orange out to the other side, so that it rolled into one's waiting hand and one got thankfully into bed, not knowing.

She found herself laughing and caught her breath, because laughter resounded so, in the silence; felt a tautening in the throat, as of hysteria, and gripped the newel post at the bottom of the stairs with her left hand, to steady herself. The white fingers, the bony knuckles standing out and the rings winking under the light, hardly looked like her own, but more like an instrument she was using as an ineffectual extension of herself. She stared at the hand, moved it so that the rings were extinguished and then flashed again, reassured herself, stood upright and breathed deeply in order to be able to send out the imperious command, to the extremities of her body, to the extremities of the house, to fall back into harmony with the rest of the universe and move in tune with it again.

'What d'you mean?' Phil was asking, 'What business? I've no idea what you're talking about.' He faced his mother across the dining-room table, a glass and a clean drying-up cloth in his hands, as if he had begun to do something and had forgotten what it was. 'You keep dropping these weird hints. What are you try-ing to say?'

His mother looked round, looking for spies and eavesdroppers, Phil thought, even here, hiding be-hind the furniture she polished each day. Her lowered

130

voice, her look reminded him of the day he had gone away to school and she had come into his room in the evening to tell him about the Facts of Life. At the time, he had thought: these are not the facts of any-body's life, let alone ours, hers and mine. He had stared out of the window then, not speaking, until she had finished. The knowledge oppressed him, then as now, that words must fall upon his ears that he did not want to hear; something whispered, vague, obscene; something irrelevant to him, and intrusive. He put down the glass and the cloth on the sideboard, finally, and lit a cigarette.

'Well, come on, out with it, Ma. It can't be that bad. Are you going to tell me I'm illegitimate or something?'

She looked at him, shocked and muddled. 'Oh, don't be so silly, Philip, I thought you asked me about Mrs Fletcher, didn't you? I don't know what on earth you're on about now.'

'No, it's not that I asked, it's just that you've been trying to tell me, dropping all these hints all the time. I'm not that nosy about other people's lives. But you've spent the whole day going on about some "business" as you call it, and now I'm just mildly curious to know what it is, and why it applies to me, as you seem to think it does.'

'Oh, I don't know. I suppose it was just on my mind today. With you popping over to see her, I suppose. It didn't seem to matter so much when you were a little boy, I didn't think you'd understand, but now you're older, I think you ought to know. No, don't joke about it, Phil, it's nothing to make light of.'

'Well, what isn't, for God's sake?'

She looked up at him again, hurt and wishing all at once that they could simply be silent. 'Well, it's just that he didn't die naturally, Mr Fletcher.'

'D'you mean, she did him in?' Flippancy was the only protection.

'Oh, no, nothing as awful as that. No, of course not. No, they think he did away with himself.'

'Oh, is *that* all.' He sighed, waving a hand as if to dismiss it, but inside felt a dim pain take root and grow.

'All?' She stared at him.

'Well, you made it sound as though it was going to be something much worse. After all, lots of people commit suicide, don't they?'

'Not round here, they don't. I don't know what goes on at your university, but people I know don't take their own lives like that, I can tell you. Things like that don't just happen for no reason, now, do they?'

'But I don't see what it's got to do with us.' He flicked his ash about, angrily. She watched the light flecks cover the carpet.

'Why on earth you can't use the ash tray, dear, it makes so much work. . . . I just thought you were old enough to know, that was all. After all, she's always taken an interest in you.'

'So I'm supposed to take an interest in her old man doing himself in? I'm supposed to click my teeth and promise never to go near her again? O.K., you think I'm old enough to know, well, I'm old enough not to want to know. I don't give a damn about it. What's past is past, and I don't know why you have to go raking it all over again. For Christ's sake. Forget it, I'm not interested.'

She sighed deeply again, a sound he knew, that he had heard from the far corners of the house all through his boyhood and that made him fret and shake his head under the angry burden. He turned away and rubbed the butt of his cigarette round and round in the ash tray, watching it go out. 'I don't care, I don't care,' he repeated in his mind. He heard himself telling Lucy, 'I don't care, I don't care.' Lucy would understand; these deep, violent feelings of his she nursed up carefully, like plants. But no, he would not tell her, for she would understand too well. He felt himself strung out like this between the two of them, hung there to be scrutinised and picked dry, piece by piece. Today was a battle, and he the field upon which the horses stamped. Lucy strained him to her, her eyes wide when he was limp and tired, her nostrils tense like those of a war horse, a little stamping charger; his mother sighed, and the sigh whispered through the rooms, stirred the curtains, hushed and persistent as the ominous wind that stirred the trees and the pennants and sent a rustle through the waiting troops. He thought of Andrew. What would Andrew do? He would do nothing, but walk on in a straight line, perceiving neither the battlefield nor the fighters. But was he what they had made of him, having calmly, gracefully given in? Or was he, Philip wondered, for the first time in his life, something else? He remembered what it had been like on the bus, being rocked along in the direction of his parents' house; those trees along the roadside, their blunt and hideous stumps raised innocently to the sky.

'Where's Andrew?' he said.

'What?' He had startled her again. She was mopping and wiping and trying to repair her make-up. He hated the dried, cracked pink of her powder compact, waved about in public. 'Andrew? I think he's helping Heather put Jojo to bed.' She sniffed. 'I heard them making a lot of noise in the bedroom a while ago. I should think he's in the bedroom with them. Why? What d'you want him for?'

'Why?' He wanted to say, I have never in my whole life spoken to my brother. I don't know who he is. But he looked at her, and could say nothing. It was as if insects were buzzing around his head, worrying at his eyes and his nostrils, settling on the corners of his mouth, avid for the mucus and the damp of his living face, clustering and buzzing and whining at his ears. He shook his head and the hair fell across his brow. Like a pony, she was thinking, suddenly outside herself for a moment, like a nervous young pony. How could she ever tell him that she loved him? All she could do was tell him not to flick ash all over the floor; now, it was too late for her even to smooth the hair out of his eyes for him, or to adjust his tie.

'Why? Well, why not?' Philip said impatiently, 'I just want to see him, that's all. You're always asking why.' He had forced himself to speak and hurt her further; it was something he had to do, to go on doing, if he was to win through today at all, if he and Lucy were to find their house and their happiness. He moved roughly past his mother, out of the room, flinging open the door that she had so carefully closed behind them when she shut them in with that

134

muffled secret; he ran up the stairs, still shaking his head to get the bees out of his ears, the words out of his mind, bounded up the stairs three at a time as if he were still a boy, as if he lived here again, as if his hand belonged on the banister and his feet lightly leaping up the stairs. He stood poised on the landing, called, 'Andrew? Andrew!' out loud, as if his voice were at home in this house, and listened, waiting, for a moment.

'What?' His brother's voice came from the bedroom he shared with Heather and the baby.

'Andrew? Come for a walk? Come to the pub?'

'What? Coming.' Andrew's long dark face came round the corner of the door, which was only opened a little. Philip felt the weight of some unguessed-at marital scene leaning upon it, so that it was hard to open.

'What did you say?'

'I said, come to the pub. Come out with me for a bit. I could do with a pint.'

'Isn't it nearly supper time? Isn't it a bit late? And won't there be something to drink here, any-way?'

'Well,' said Philip, waving his hands, dancing about on the landing, 'it won't be supper time yet, it's only about half seven and I've seen Mum in the kitchen and she's not ready yet. Come on, it'll do us good to get out. Get a bit of a walk. I've done nothing but eat today, and there's another huge meal coming up, by the looks of things.'

'O.K. But what about you, darling?' he called back to Heather. 'Will you be all right? I won't be gone long.'

'Don't come home blotto,' returned the dry, calm voice of Heather.

Phil could imagine her sitting in there, her small hands deftly buttoning up the supine baby, her dark eyes unfathomable. Who was she? What were they to each other? What went on beneath the calmness of their rippled surface, in the dark places where the weeds swam? He stared at Andrew curiously as his brother came out of the bedroom. All the familiar things, the hard-edged, the certain, began to merge, their colours layered and dimmer than they were, all known shapes melted and became strange to each other, all sound was distorted as the cry that rises from a tunnel. Andrew was as mysterious as a traveller dust-stained from a foreign land, leaving casually as he did that bedroom where his wife and child remained, he was remote as a man whose consciousness lies in the firm hands of a drug. They exchanged a glance, as they descended the stairs, and there was wariness in it, and curiosity, and some friendliness. Phil thought, if I met him in the street I don't know that I would recognise him. Andrew thought, there is something in this, he wants something, he has come to me armed and yet pleading, bearing a threat, and yet I go willingly. They both thought, and yet he is my brother.

'Are you sure they're open?' Andrew said in the silence.

'Yes, of course, it's after seven. Come on, I've got some cash. No, don't go explaining to everybody, it's all right. Come on, let's go.'

Lucy, unknown to the rest of the household, sat in

the study, a book upon her knees. This room bore no marks of anybody studying in it except for the books, all of them twenty years old and more, their jackets bound in the dull blues and reds of the early years of the century or done in the scruffy war-time way with torn covers and pages that smelt peculiar and felt coarse. People had studies to tell the world that their minds were not yet dead, whatever appearances might suggest. They had stacks of books, and pretended to have read them. They read a few, snipped a few ideas out of them, pasted the cuttings in the scrapbooks of their minds and produced them, yellowed and fading, to show off to company in twenty years' time. Her father, though, really had a study and really had a mind. She felt, sitting in this cold unvisited room with the cheap novels of 1928 around her, a sudden longing to be at home, away from all this pretence. Their house in London might be a mess, and maybe guests did have to go without loo paper and make do with the *Guardian* instead – a circumstance which, when it happened, filled her with fury – but at least there were things in it that were real. She saw in her mind the tattered hall, the pot plant on a dusty table, the heap of books done up in brown paper that had arrived a couple of days ago for her father to review, and which were still waiting to be opened. There was the hall mirror, handsome and gilt, but with spots on its face, there was her father's mac hanging on a peg, and his galoshes – why wear galoshes in London, she asked him – that lay haphazard below it, where he had kicked them off. The dog's lead lay on the hall table, beside the books, and a pair of dirty old string gloves with it, their blunt fingers curling round, the shape of her father's hands; he must have been taking the dog for a walk in the park, and it was raining. There would be dog footprints all through the house; she heard the rattle of wet claws on lino, smelt the rough smell of wet hair. There were many things that were appalling about her father's house in London. When she was there, she attacked him for his vagueness, letting the fire go out, leaving the front door open so that the wind took all the letters and bills from the mat and scattered them over the area railings and a strange dog came and peed in the hall; and for his untidiness, his hopelessness, his incompetence, his forgotten meals and lost appointments. No butter at breakfast and no paper in the loo drove her at him furiously. And the coldness of the bedrooms and there being no sheets left in the linen cupboard because they were all still parcelled and waiting at the launderette for the moment when he had some spare cash, for all the world as if they were at a pawn shop. These things, she told herself, were not so important; and after all, if she really minded, she could always fetch the laundry and buy the butter and order the loo paper herself. But still, he could afford a housekeeper, as well as that woman who came late in the mornings and stood around breathing reverently over the books. And she, after all, was only down from college for a few weeks at a time. It was his house, and he ought to look after it, just as he ought to look after himself and not, in that vague slutty way of his, let himself go to pieces when he was only forty-nine. She was always brushing and tidying him, telling him he ought to shave before going out to lunch, mocking at him for the egg on his tie and the nicotine that stained his fingers almost to the wrist, because, as she told him, 'It might be today that you meet the rich widow. And then you'd be sorry.' The rich widow was her invention, and she used her to batter and cajole him. Sometimes, it was a matter of praying that the rich widow would come and deliver her, sometimes that the rich widow and all she stood for would simply disappear. But in her heart, she knew that she did not exist. He would not marry again; he was too lazy, too bored with other people, too immersed in his work. The rich widow would only stand a chance if she were both an expert on the Tudor price rise and content to be lectured on it endlessly; if she assiduously tidied and decorated the house and then were prepared to let it run to seed; if she cared about clothes and jewellery and could yet love a man with egg on his tie. Her own mother had been one of those, and had died in the attempt; there would not be another like her. So, with an occasional sigh of love and exasperation, she had come to terms, nearly, with the knowledge that her father would eventually depend on her for everything. There would be perhaps years of freedom, years in which she could marry and work and have her own life, but there, waiting at the end of the line, was the day on which her father, old, weak and alone, still muttering about the price rise, would summon her back; and there she would be, back in the squalor she had fought against for so long, back with the long silent mealtimes, the cold food, the cold rooms, the mounting piles of old newspapers which could not be thrown away in case they were important, the heaps of books which could not be put away, because he was using them. There would be the dog hair on one's clothes, the damp dripping walks in the park, the railings to be counted as she had counted them as a child, the mac and the galoshes in the hall. There would be her own exasperation and tenderness, intensified now, because he was old; she would be there, engulfed at last in the constricting world of her childhood and girlhood; and university, freedom, love, Philip, all these would be shown to be ephemeral, a passing, beautiful dream. And it was no good people telling her that there were home helps and meals-on-wheels and homes for old people, or even mentioning euthanasia, because that would not be the point. Fatalistically, this she knew.

It was strange, how one had to come away from things to find their worth. Here, in this drab little room with its olive walls and ugly light wooden furniture, she found a grandeur in her father's life that she had never seen so completely. Among these unread books and piles of old colour supplements, she felt the force and beauty of his obsession with an old, obscure subject; here, among these edgy, raucous people, she appreciated the quiet he wore about him, the carelessness of other people's opinions, the air of lonely delapidation. She thought, after this I will go home. Whatever happens, I will go home. And there was hardly room for Phil, while this thought flooded her mind, although it had been on his account that she had sought out this lonely seat by the bookshelves and had sat here, thumbing and wondering. For however she might wish to pin him there, at the centre of her life, this boy, her friend and lover, it was yet

impossible. He was too shadowy, too evasive. She
needed to place him there, and say: I depend upon
you utterly; she willed herself to say it, found the
words ready in her mouth, yet could not believe them
enough even to say them in solitude. He eluded her,
and as he moved and shuddered and vacillated under
her grip, fighting her off, she felt ever more real and
present in her mind the battered house in London
and the lonely, independent, aging man who lived
there. The book on her knees now was an old family
photograph album, pulled out from beneath a heap
of magazines on the bottom shelf. On the first page
was a picture of Philip as a baby. Deliberately, she
began to turn the pages and examine each one.

That year, the winter nights were sodden, black and
windless. No frost on the ground, none whitening the
twigs, even in January, no patterned window-panes
nor crystalline late mornings, breaking into brilliant
blue. The rain fell, day and night, gentle on the
leaves that were glued like papier-mâché, making a
footfall quiet in the drenched garden. Trees stood
and drooped under the rain, black branches of a
beech gleamed in the fickle light of early day, apple
boughs were twisted, matt and furrowed, and in the
grass between the trees apples turned to pulp. The
path from the house to the potting shed was slippery
and overgrown, tall dead weeds, sticks only, stood in
its way. The roof of the shed poured with cross-
channels of water, a fall of water ploughed the earth
from the broken gutter, the drainpipe stood crooked
beside the shed, held awkwardly like a fractured arm.
    In one of the houses, a child cried in the night,

and its mother rose blind with sleep and fumbled her
way to feed it, once in the cruel small hours after
midnight, and again at six, when morning was still
only a far-off promise and the sky was black and
dense, the room as cold as ever. Boiled milk over-
flowed and burned on an old stove; somebody swore,
for milk was still precious and the stove was a pest
to clean. There was a cat asleep in the lap of a
kitchen chair, but its animal warmth was all the
warmth there was in that chill room, for until the
frost came, until it was real winter, to light the fires
would be a waste. The young mother flapped back to
bed in her slippers, feeling the unusual weight still
of her breasts and stomach under her dressing-gown.
The near part of the double bed was still warm and
printed with the shape of her body; she got into it
and huddled into her own outline, her own foetal
shape; but the rest of the bed was cold, empty, an
unexplored territory; her hands could stretch across
it and find no edge, no solid thing, just the frightening cold expanse of sheet. The baby in its cot had the
sheets and blankets tucked tight around its ears, so
that only a domed, furred head and a wrinkled nose
emerged. Under the wrappings, the fists clenched as
they had so recently in the womb. There was silence
throughout the house again, beneath the weight of
the rain upon the roof, but the young mother's sleep
was uneasy and she had to peer several times at her
watch to make sure that it was not yet six, and listen
intently in the dark to hear her baby's breathing,
which seemed still such a miracle. She turned and
turned in the bed, clutching the blankets closer to
her to wrap in some warmth around her cold, tired

limbs and shut out the expanses, the emptiness. And through the slight patter of the rain and the thick dark, she heard a creak and a click, as of a door closing; she sat up, all faculties straining, the wakeful tenseness of all the war years returning to her instantly. Rain, rain, blotting up sound, distorting all movement to the fumbling of a blind man's foot; and yet, a sudden clarity – yes, she heard it, she was sure – the clarity of steps upon a path, feet that knew even in the rain and dark where they were going and would not hesitate; somebody was walking across the garden, it sounded close enough to be her garden, walking away from the house, in which a door had been opened and closed, and away from her. There was a click, a latch lifting, and another, louder, creak; this door was stiffer, heavier, harder to open than the last; and the final closing was the last sound for the moment that she heard. Again the rain pattered, nothing but the rain tapping upon the roof, and her intense listening made patterns of it that repeated themselves in her mind. The silence was long, complete, under the rain. She felt the earth, the whole land around her, saturated with the rain; everything had become spongy, absorbent; she was like a sponge too, all receptivity, soaking up the endless, impossible amount of water, and the incessant repetition of the sound. And then the silence and the rain were split by the sudden, appalling shock – the explosion of pure sound that made the darkness flower in sparks of red and purple, spattered blood upon the dark passivity of the universe, turned the walls to vivid paintings, which were there when the sound was gone, and would be there always, as again

and again the crack split the night, again and again
the flesh and blood of a man became paint, spraying
the smooth surface of the world, marking indelibly
those four blank walls, and again and again the waiting consciousness of the one who was forced to listen
reeled under that blow; the flowers of orange and red
and purple grew and spread slowly against the back-
cloth of night, the sound died away, and the flowers
were left to fade while the breathless, waiting listening went on, hands clutched the bedclothes, eyes
strained to pierce the dark, a hundred, thousand ears
were listening, right across the part of the world that
was in darkness, it seemed. And then there was nothing; but after that moment of absolute nullity, in the
dark, the angry cry rose from a child that had been
woken up and was hungry. And then it was as if the
cry released all the other cries, for somewhere somebody was sobbing, hard, uncomfortable sobs that
blocked the throat, as if all the truth in the world had
been betrayed, so that there was no hope.

5

Philip put down his beer mug after the first long swig and said, 'It's a house all by itself, set back from the road, with a tree by the gate. Near Sutton. Well, quite near. But it's what we want. You know?' He had found it impossible not to tell his brother about the house, and now, as he told, he was begging him for approval and confirmation.

'But?' Andrew had said, but the money, but the remoteness, but the unpracticality of it all. His objections hung between them like fog.

Phil said, 'But you must understand why one wants things, why one has to do things.'

'Me?'

'Yes, I mean, you got married, you had a child, you did what you wanted. Well, I want to marry Lucy and live there.'

'But Phil, there are differences in kinds of wanting. Aren't there?' he said. 'The possible and the impossible, surely. I might as well say I wanted to take a trip round the world, and set off tomorrow, and expect the money to appear from somewhere. Or run a ranch in Arizona, or be a tycoon or something. You're still at the engine-driver stage. You can't just shout for things and expect them to be there.'

Phil said, 'But it's not a difference in kind, only in degree. All those things only sound impossible in financial terms. Morally, there's nothing to stop you. I mean, being who you are doesn't prevent you. If you wanted to do any of those things enough, you could. It only needs effort. The trouble is your desire to do them doesn't match up to the amount of effort you would need. Well,' he paused and sipped his beer, 'you see, mine does. So I can do it, the thing I want. It may not sound so ambitious, just wanting to go and live in an old house in the country, but it's what I want. We've got a certain amount of money, we can buy it if Dad gives us the go-ahead, and when the loot runs out, I'll sell books and vegetables.'

'Dad? Can you see him agreeing to a scheme like that?' Phil remembered now what his brother looked like when he was scornful; his eyes puckered at the corners, the edges of his mouth turned down. 'And besides, you'd be so busy patching up the house and looking after the place, you wouldn't have time to write books, would you, let alone grow enough

146

vegetables to sell. It's all so bloody Utopian. I can't see you living like that, really. And what about Lucy? What would she do in a place like that? Weave home-made skirts?'

Phil looked past him, at the bar with its distant rows of glasses. 'She wants it. She wants to go there as much as I do. We've had enough of it, this life that you lead here, that Mum and Dad live. All the rub-bish, you know. Jobs, commuting, filthy shitty towns, trees chopped down, people chopped, everybody getting fucked up, nothing natural or living or real. We've just had it, we're blowing, getting the hell out. We want a different sort of life, a place where our kids can grow up without getting all fucked up like we were. Well, it's the only thing you can do, isn't it? Well, can you honestly say you're happy? I mean, I don't know, but it must be pretty shitty. Mum and Dad on your back the whole time, sweat-ing away at a job all day, no time for yourself, your little house in a row of little houses, backwards and forwards every day, and a lousy pension at the end of it?'

'It's not like that,' Andrew said. 'Really it isn't. You don't know the first thing about my life.'

'Sorry. I suppose I shouldn't have gone on about it. I suppose I get you mixed up with the parents in my mind. It's just that superficially at least you seem to have opted for the same deal. And I want something else. I'm getting it, too. Lucy's right, you have to stop waiting around for people to give you things – here, boy, here's your little grant, don't spend it all in the same shop and if you throw any naughty bombs we'll take it away again. You have to take. It's happening everywhere, at last. The Black Power people are right. The world's not going to give you anything, kid, if you just sit around looking hopeful. All you get from that is a sore arse from sitting at an office desk all your life, and maybe ulcers and impotence thrown in. Lucy's right, it's a new scene. Me first, if you like. You can't be any good to anyone, mate, if you aren't getting what you need yourself. You're just a cripple, like most of the people we know, like our parents' generation, all loused up with sacrifice and patriotism and honour and glory and dying for the flag, if you don't honestly, seriously, consider what kind of thing you need for yourself. You know, I think they just fought that war really because they were so shit-scared of finding a Jerry in the back garden snipping through the garden fence with his little tweezers and pulling up the roses. Not for all their saving the world from the hooded menace. It was just their little skins they were saving, same as it would've been if it'd been me and you, only they wouldn't admit it, because it wouldn't sound too good. But I really admire the people who wouldn't, they at least made some decision for themselves. They knew what was right for them, they weren't going to let some superior officer take care of their lives for them and give them nothing in return. Oh, shit, I don't want to throw bombs really, or even build barricades or shout at people. I just want my own life, the way I want it. God, it ought to be an ordinary enough request, but somehow people treat you as if you're mad. What you're really supposed to do is slave for the Civil Service all your life and sit with a mortgage hanging round your neck, and insurance

148

to pay and votes to vote for some bastard you don't believe in and goodies to provide for your wife and children, only nothing, nothing for yourself, nothing for your whole bloody life except dissatisfaction and shame at the end of it. You know, has it ever struck you, Andrew,' new thoughts flooded every moment into his brain, he stammered, he flowed on again, he was eloquent, 'has it ever struck you what a thoroughly shitty deal a man gets in this society? That we're bled, gutted, castrated, snipped into little pieces and all supposedly by our own choice? I've had it, I tell you. I want men's emancipation. And Lucy agrees with me.'

The men, the glasses, the furniture of the pub, the noise around him of the talk and laughter of others, all dissolved around him and he was oblivious of them all as he talked, talking to himself as much as to Andrew, chasing the fleeting vision of a new strength for himself as he pursued the errant lines of his mind around unforeseen corners.

'Christ' was all Andrew said for a moment, as he sipped his beer and his eyes evaded Phil's but searched the company around him. 'But, O.K., maybe you're right about all that, I don't know. But how are you going to get this precious house of yours? I mean, practically?'

'I shall tell Dad what I want to do. The money is mine, really, after all. And if he refuses, I shall present him with an alternative.'

'What alternative?'

'Well. What d'you think Ma would feel like, if I never came to see them again?'

'You bastard, you aren't serious! You know what'd

happen. She lives for you coming. She'd go crazy, God knows why, but she would. But you couldn't do it, Phil. It's blackmail, and bloody cruel blackmail too. But it's just not you. You aren't like that; you couldn't do it.' He stared at Phil curiously, across the little table. 'Did Lucy put you up to this?'

'No!' he muttered. 'No, she didn't. You seem to think I've no mind of my own. But you're right, I wouldn't do it. Not really. But God, Andrew,' he raised his head and gazed at his brother, challenging, despairing, 'it's not from any feelings of love, or anything like that, nothing real. It's just that I'm tied, by duty, fear, or whatever you like. They've just got me hamstrung. That's what I meant at lunch. The immorality of the régime. You know, all those beautiful memories of our childhood, repeated again and again until we believe them, when really it was awful; and we have to defeat them to be free, prove they're lies, or we'll never even be people. D'you know what I'm talking about?'

Andrew's eyes, he thought, were opaque; one could tell nothing, for the depths were veiled. 'I've felt it all day, that I had to talk to you, somehow to get things straight. Come on, let's have another pint.' He lit a cigarette, to indicate that he was here for as long as Andrew would stay with him. 'It was so blatant at lunch. It's like *Brave New World* or something. Sometimes I don't think they even know themselves that they're lies. They grow and grow, things like that. The past turns into a sort of solid, indestructible thing, and yet it's only made of bits from the past, selected bits, carefully picked out and glued together with sentiment. It's like giving somebody a jigsaw puzzle of the Royal Family and saying, this is life. I've got to do something about it. I realised it today, I think, when Lucy and I were walking up from the bus stop, along that god-awful road, Rosebery Avenue, or whatever it's called. I've just got to break it open. That's why I felt a minute ago that I could blackmail them, threaten them, do anything, if it would only get me freedom. I can't get married like this, Andrew, that's what it is. You must know what I'm on about. I don't think Lucy quite understands, she's convinced it's quite easy to be free, she thinks all I have to do is turn up here and announce what I'm going to do and tell them all to get stuffed. But it's not that easy. Well, I suppose it is for her, she's only got a civilised old father, he's a don or something and he doesn't give a damn what Lucy does anyway. But me, look at me, the bloody prodigal son, and what am I going to do about it? Help me, go on, for God's sake buy me another drink and tell me your side of it, tell me you remember the tyranny and the humiliation and the god-awful stinking bourgeois pettiness of our sanctified home life. Go on, you're older than me, you can remember more, you knew what was happening to me when I was a baby, when I was little, you can see it all from the point of view of the jealous elder brother – you were jealous, you hated me, don't you remember? Hating your curly-headed sweet little baby brother? Mummy's pet? The kid who always got what he wanted, as long as it was what they wanted him to have? Because if you'll admit that, then we're getting somewhere. Tell me, do you hate me now? Do you wish I'd never been born? Go on, help me, Andrew, for God's sake.

You must be on my side, you must understand. Do you? Or do you think I'm mad?'

Lucy and Heather moved about the supper table, adjusting a fork here, adding a pepper pot there, with the slightly haughty air of women who think their men have been too long in the pub. They had both come to offer help in the first place because there had been such banging and slamming from the kitchen; Felicity, when they entered, looked up at them quickly, as though to say, I haven't a minute to spare, so say what you want to and get it over with, and don't pretend you really want to help because I don't believe it. Lucy thought, her mind still partly anchored to the house in London, thank goodness there is nobody in my life who is a permanent martyr, nobody to say, Now, look what you've made me do; thank goodness this cloying feeling of guilt is not one that I often feel. Heather said nothing, did not look up at Lucy as they passed each other, scrupulously, to take knives out of the drawer; but there was something about the movement of her hands and about the incline of her head that suggested a deep, hardly perceptible insolence. She was like an Arab woman, like a picture of an Arab woman; her gliding movements, her pussyfoot walk, soft voice, glowing averted eyes were all the attributes of submissiveness; and yet, one felt it would be easy for her to draw herself to attention, turn those eyes fully and spit in the dust at one's feet. She was like an Arab serving girl with a bomb in her pocket, waiting for the revolution. Lucy watched her covertly, and felt herself angular and awkward by comparison. Heather was ancient, she was archetypal. And so, why Andrew, why Sundays here, why the pose as the loving and submissive daughter-in-law? Why was she not alone in some desert place, gathering the tribute of men's eyes?

Lucy stood back, heard the clock on the mantelpiece tick and thought, Why don't they come back? Here I am lost, abandoned, out of my depth. I don't want to be here, and yet here I am, laying the table with two strange women, and Phil has put me here. Anger rose in her – anger at the silence, at the impending supper, at the ugly room, littered with newspapers, the lights, the house, the street; anger at Phil's mother and the inscrutable Heather, anger particularly at Phil himself. She had come here to help him to reject the place, so that they might be free; and here she was, embroiled already in trivial domestic situations, while they tried to assimilate her as if she were assimilable, as if she already fitted in. She glared at Heather in passing. Why could she not give a hint, a sign? Why must she be at once so mysterious and so trivial? One could surprise Heather outside in the corridor, as she went up to see if her little boy were asleep, one could seize her by the arm and shake her, and say, what is it? One could force her to explain. But no, one could do neither. Lucy saw already those dark eyes, retreating, that opaque, beautiful mask staring back, in polite surprise. Heather would pass on down the passage, freeing herself, insulting with her discreetly masked hint of outrage. One would get nowhere.

She said, 'Whatever can they have got up to? They must be completely canned by now.' Her voice sounded brittle.

Heather said, 'Yes, it does seem a long time, doesn't it? But in fact they've only been gone forty minutes.'

Felicity said, 'I can't think why they have to go and rush off to the pub, just when supper's ready. There's plenty of beer here, too.'

Silence was resumed. Then Heather said, 'Well, I expect they've got a lot to talk about. And they'd hardly want us listening in to it all, would they?' Lucy gave her a long look through her hair, but the smooth face gave nothing away.

It was then that they all three heard a crash, somewhere outside; at least, Lucy jumped and cried 'What was that?' certain that the others must have heard it too. 'What was it? What happened?' she appealed, darting from one to the other in her agitation, shocked out of her thoughts as though a bell had rung loudly in her ear, waking her somewhere where she should not have fallen asleep. She thought all at once of Phil – something could have happened to Phil – remembering uneasily the way they had parted, how she had said, 'Oh, well, do what you like, I don't care;' how her passionate love had turned in half an hour to anger, and now to unease. She dropped a dish noisily on the table, 'What was it? Somebody's outside, somebody's crashed something, do you think someone is hurt? It sounded so close, as if it were in the garden.'

'It could have been a car door,' Heather said, watching her.

'Oh, surely not in our garden?' Felicity, drying her hands with swift agitation upon her apron, untying the strings, standing in the doorway already in defence. 'You don't think it was, do you, Lucy?

Surely it must have been something in the road? Yes, Heather's probably right, it probably was a car door. Although it didn't really sound like a car door.'

'Not so metallic,' said Lucy. 'And not in the direction of the road.'

'Oh, you don't think it was somebody . . . dropping something? That somebody could have been about to break in? One of you, go and ask Daddy if he heard it. Ask him to go and see. Oh, dear, I do wish the boys were back, they are so late.' They stood, the three of them, uncomfortably united in their indecision, and no sound, no explanation came to them. They shivered, and glanced at each other, and for a second it was as if their hands might go out to each other, hand grasp hand in reassurance, the affirmation of human warmth cancel all calculation; but none of them moved closer to the others, and the moment was gone, the chill passed, like a small cloud. Lucy got out her crumpled packet of cigarettes from her pocket, and offered them round, as if there had been an air raid, she thought, or they had been stuck in a lift, but neither of them accepted so she smoked alone.

'I don't see that digging up the past can do much good,' Andrew was saying. 'Surely it's the present that matters, what one actually feels at the moment?'

'Yes, but the past has a horrid sort of grip on us, doesn't it? On us particularly, because what we're allowed to see is a phoney past. It's like a kind of home movie. Mum and Dad and the two kids frolicking on the bright green lawn, with faithful Rover licking his chops in the background.'

'Yes, the dog. They were wrong about that. I give you that. But one could hardly say it, at lunch.'

'They were bloody wrong. Well, you see what I mean, don't you?'

'Well, I see that they had to invent it all,' Andrew said, 'because they're so bloody miserable now. Because they can't stand not having had a happy past to gloat over, so they invent one, they allow themselves to see it all different because otherwise life would be intolerable. They weren't happy then and they aren't happy now, and those home movies are simply all they've got. So don't take it away from them. Because it's cruel, and unnecessary. Just let them think we loved it all, let them hang on to their picture of us frolicking on the lawn. So what, we never frolicked, but then, come to think of it, there's not much proven truth about most religions.'

Phil was silent, and sat there rubbing his hands over his eyes as if he were suddenly quite exhausted.

'I see,' he said. 'That's why you wouldn't admit it, was it? I thought you'd gone over to the enemy. But you were just giving them a bit of quarter.'

'Well, just think,' Andrew said, and they lit their last two cigarettes, 'think of arriving at the end of one's life, fully conscious that you had neither been happy yourself nor made anybody else happy. Do you grudge them the home movies they want to keep playing over to themselves before that happens? Do you blame them for wanting to avoid that conscious-ness? Mum will just think of all the happy birthdays she's had, and Dad will think of how he always re-membered them and bought a present in time. That's all. It doesn't hurt you. It seems harmless enough.'

156

'Hmm.'

'Whereas us,' he went on, 'you and me, we've got a hell of a lot of time left to us, I hope. We've got time to choose, and change things, make sure we are happy. You said that yourself. It's okay to demand things, now. It's okay to say, me first. But them, they didn't have a chance. Shit, they didn't even have a chance to find out who they were and where they lived before they were slap-bang in the middle of a bloody war, shooting hell out of a bunch of other kids on the other side of Europe. They didn't have a chance. They couldn't say, me first, and this is what I want, and I want to live in a big house in the country and nobody bugging me please. All they had, as far as I can see, was falling into bed with each other while the bombs dropped all around them, quick, before somebody got his head or his balls shot off, **and then us, all the kids** born in the horrible 1940s who grew up into grey flannel trousers and jerseys knitted with the wool from Uncle So-and-so's old jersey that he won't need any more, because he was bashed on the head in France and he's not coming back; us, they had us in spite of all that, because it was the only thing they could do, when all around you are losing theirs the only thing you can do is fuck, right? And here we are. And then there was peace, and they thought maybe they'd got the wrong person on the other side of the bed, after all, but by that time it was too late and everybody was burning their ration books and saying, this is your life, this is what you fought for, now you've got to like it. See what I mean?'

'I never knew you felt like that. Funny, isn't it.'

'Funny?'

'Peculiar. Odd. That I never knew you thought that. D'you know,' he tipped the drains of his beer down, and sighed, 'together, I mean, if we'd been one person, we could have been somebody. Don't you think? Come on, man, we'd better go home.'

Felicity heard the front door open; the boys were in the hall, she heard them stamp about and laugh, throwing down their coats. They came in, noisy and pink in the face, like gay intruders.

'Phil,' said Lucy at once. 'There was a tremendous crash outside. Did you hear it? D'you know what it was?'

'It wasn't really a very tremendous crash,' Heather said.

'No,' he said, 'I didn't hear anything. But we were talking. When was it, anyway? Oh, I shouldn't think it was anything, would you?'

'You are late, you two boys,' Felicity said. 'This soup's been ready for hours, I can't think what you were doing, all this time. I do think you might have a little more consideration. Making us wait all this time for our supper. You're lucky there's any for you at all. Now, go and call your father, Philip, and tell him it's ready. If we don't eat now, the whole evening will be gone. I've been cooking meals, I've been on my feet all day, and I think I might be allowed a little time to sit down.'

'It's only just after eight,' Andrew said, 'but you sit down, Mum, I'll dish it out. Go on, sit down and have a drink or something. Leave the rest to us. Phil, will you call Dad?'

'Phil,' said Lucy, 'Do you think. . . ?'

158

'Oh, don't fuss, love,' he said, 'sit down and have some supper. No, of course it wasn't anything. You lot seem to have got yourselves thoroughly worked up while we've been away.' And she heard him at the foot of the stairs, calling, 'Dad? Dad? Supper's ready,' and with a sigh, sat down to drink her soup.

In her seat beside the droning gas fire, Mrs Fletcher sat tensed for a moment, listening. It was a high wail that she had heard, a cry from the dark, from somewhere beyond the warm, lighted room that contained herself, her supper tray, her carefully created Sunday evening peace. She held herself taut, listened for it again. There it came, a cry of anguish and fear; surely the cry of a very young cat, stuck somewhere where it did not want to be. Strange that when she heard it, that high, wild cry from outside, she should forget her unease about the far corners of the house and the rustling undergrowth of the unkempt garden. It must be a cat, she thought, a cat stuck up a tree, on a roof, even on a chimney-pot, a cat too young and gormless to find its own way down; what was one to do? Perhaps if one went upstairs and called from a window, it might be able to get in across the roof? Or if it were up a tree. . . . She went to the front door, opened it wide, stared out into the glittering September night and stood very small beside the trees that stretched their branches to the stars, calling, 'Puss? Puss-puss? Kitty-kitty-kitty? Come on then, poor thing, tell me where you are, come on, kitty-cat, kitty-cat, puss, puss, puss?'

Silence, then a faint mew, from somewhere high up. That meant that it knew help was on the way and yet was determined to sound as pathetic as possible, perhaps to hurry things up; self-conscious beasts they were! Smiling a little, she stood in the porch and listened again. There! It was in the plum tree that grew close to the house. Not too high up, by the sound of it. If she were to go up on to the landing, and open the window and call it from there, it should be able to creep along a branch, get on to the roof, and leap in through the landing window to safety.

She did not stop to wonder whose cat it was, nor what she would do with it once it was rescued, but set off up the stairs, intent on her purpose. On the landing she stood for a minute, listening, and began then to fumble with the window, pushing the curtain aside. It was hard to push the sash up, this one was hardly ever opened; it was stiff, she was stiff; she stood on tiptoe and pushed, and the backs of her legs and her arms ached with the effort. At last the sash swung up and the night cold air rushed in. Silence and darkness. The twigs of the plum tree reached out for the house, tapped and rattled at the gutters; there was a branch, thin and twiggy where it touched the roof, as far as she could see, and then the gutter, and then a slippery stretch of roof, up to the window-sill. It was rotten, that gutter, it should have been mended, and there was that stain on the wall of the house because of it, and the damp creeping in. She stretched until the tension ran right down from fingertip to toe, a wire upon which an old body hung, she clutched the sill with both hands and peered out into the night; there were the lights of the house next door, through the trees, supper being eaten, a warm room and young voices remote now as sounds travel-

160

ling in space; calling, her voice was so thin, nobody would ever hear but perhaps a cat. 'Puss, puss, puss! Come on then, this way, come on, just a little way up, come on, puss, puss, puss!' A rattle, a scrabble of twigs and bark as if something fell and then caught on to the tree with fragile claws and hung there, clutching for a foothold, the damp pieces of bark falling all around it; a thin shriek and a crash; the cat had fallen into the gutter, had regained its balance, was coming gingerly, with frantic relieved mews, up the roof, outlined black against the silver dampness under the moon; and then there was the crash, the door slamming upon sanity, cutting off the world, she was caught, severed from her own extremities as the unspeakable pain flowed up her arms, then she was hanging, sobbing, screaming, the noise she made remote and useless, and her heart was pounding as the pain flowed through and came to it, jolting like an old tree struck in a storm; pain rushed, seized, like a brief light flashed upon the world, and she saw in that light that her hands were out there incomprehensibly apart from her so that fire leapt and blazed in her wrists and could find no escape; she saw against the glass in the sudden clarity the dumb screaming face of the cat, its eyes like lamps, its mouth a wide pink maw, she understood at last what had happened; and with understanding came release, the jolting shuddered to a stop, something fluttered and leapt and was still at last. The little cat stayed on the window-sill, its mouth opening and shutting in cry after cry, its claws and its breath scarring the solid glass, yet was neither heard nor seen.

*

Doors slam in the mind, barring out sanity; doors swing and a certain course of action is forever on the other side; a point in life is past, never to be regained. One never goes back to the point of not knowing what came afterwards. The time that rules men's minds runs perhaps like a coil, but the generations are beads threaded upon it and nobody can step past the next or past the previous one. All our elasticity cannot reach out to understand, to assimilate, to prevent. We jostle each other and touch, but are enclosed each in our hard shell, circular and smooth, strung on the line which stretches mindlessly in both directions. There are similarities, there are hints, there are moments when one drowns in the delusion of love and power, moments again when one floats to the surface and comes face to face with the pitiless sky and all the inhuman, accusing, inorganic things; and then again, moments when all stops, the movement of water, the movement of air, when one denies the whole universe with the cry, 'If only. . .' There is always the illusion that it could have been otherwise. And then there is also the enclosing shell, the bead on the string, the remorseless self. To have avoided this, I would have had to be somebody else. So Lucy thought, when she heard that Mrs Fletcher was dead.

That particular door had slammed. The window had come down on Mrs Fletcher's hands and had cut her off from the cool night air and the breath of wind and the cry of the little cat that they had found still crying on the window-sill, that morning. The window had come down because it was not one that she often used, and because the sash cord was rotten; the win-

dow had come down because there had been nobody
to help her, because she was alone.

The Ridgleys – and the Ridgleys now had to in-
clude herself – had sat down to their supper and had
eaten soup and toast and meat and potato and salad
and cheese and fruit. Their evening had been ordinary enough. They had watched the news on television
and she and Phil had walked down to the pub, put
their sixpences into the slot machine of the telephone
and told the farmer's wife that they would definitely
have the house. Then they sat one on each side of a
red formica table-top and drank down their glasses
of Guinness rather quickly, so that their absence
would not be noticed. It had been quite early when
they went upstairs to lie separately on their stiff white
little beds at opposite ends of the house. How many
hours long was a night? How many hours had
dragged out in the darkness for Mrs Fletcher before
her heart collapsed, like the broken sash cord, and
death had closed upon her? What colour was pain in
the darkness, what shape was time? And did life stay
within in the body, or did it flutter in and out, a dove
around its dovecote, in and out through the apertures,
battering and beating its wings? Did it slide quietly
away with the dawn, or was it taken savagely in the
night-time in the claws of some creature? Lucy saw
Mrs Fletcher, her arms pinned to a high window,
hanging limply while a white bird dipped its wings
and pouted its chest and fluttered all around her. She
put her elbows on the table and began to cry. It had
been the milkman who had found her.

'A heart attack,' the doctor had said. 'Probably
quite soon after it happened. She hadn't a strong

heart, you see, and it's not really surprising a shock like that killed her. Lord, the things that can happen in people's own houses. But then, she wouldn't have anybody to live in. It's nonsense, living all alone at her age. But then, you can't tell them.'

Lucy half listened, her eyes averted, as he was telling Mrs Ridgley all this. It was natural that he should have come to the Ridgleys; they, after all, were her nearest neighbours, they might have had some idea. They were the kind of people doctors did talk to after accidents, for they had the right look of concern, disapproval and tact; it was easy for them to furrow their brows and look quickly from side to side before they spoke in careful undertones. They were the natural survivors of disasters, yet they needed like a tonic its impact upon their lives. So Lucy thought, when she heard that Mrs Fletcher was dead.

'Of course, you knew that her husband killed himself,' Phil's mother was saying as she showed the doctor out. 'That must have been an awful shock. Poor old thing, she can't have had much of a life since then. Pretty lonely, I should imagine. I can't think why more old people don't like the idea of those homes. You know, the sort where they all have their own little flat and can entertain each other. I'm sure that's what I shall do.'

'Yes, well. Thank you so much. I must be on my way.'

'But surely,' said Mrs Ridgley, 'she would have known, wouldn't she? I mean, he must have had a gun. And getting out of bed and going down the garden in the middle of the night with a gun?' Going down the garden in the middle of the night with a gun. Lucy caught her breath and saw a tremor pass across Mrs Ridgley's face; the skin was drawn as though part of her was already paralysed, and the fine lines under her eyes fell away down her flat cheeks like furrows in sandy soil. Mrs Ridgley patted her hair and steadied herself by gripping an object that was hers, the round slippery knob of the front door presenting itself to her hand, solid, a tactile comfort; but there was still the figure with the gun, slipping from a bedroom, still the night, the cold, the dark, the expanse of sheet cold and untouched, the noise of wet cracking sticks and trampled under-growth, the silence of a garden under rain, spoilt by the sound of footsteps, the person out there, about to do something; and then, the shot; the blood beat in her ears as if they had only just been shocked by the noise, out there, now; she trembled and turned away from Lucy's gaze.

The doctor had not noticed. Then, 'Careful, Mrs Ridgley!' he exclaimed, seeing her sway and turn pale before him, and his arm came out to seize her before she fell so that she hung from his grip like a sack, and was propped in the doorway, and in a minute opened her eyes. 'Get some water, please,' the doctor said to Lucy, and Lucy ran.

'So he killed himself,' she said to Phil, later, her voice high and accusing. 'And you knew, did you? When did you know? And did you know he went down the garden with a gun and blew his brains out in the potting shed? Just think, just imagine, lying there, knowing. With the bed still warm where he had been, the sheets still all ruffled up and hearing him going down the garden, and waiting, and then

hearing it, the shot. Oh, I don't think I can bear
it!'

'But what,' he said, holding her forearms in both
his hands, his grip tight upon her, 'what d'you mean,
knowing. Who said anything about knowing? I don't
know what you mean. Where did you get this idea?
Lucy!'

'Oh,' she cried, 'of course she knew! She must have
known, how could she not? Imagine! Of course one
would know! But oh, Phil, after everything, after
defeating conventions and doing what they felt was
right and not fighting in the war and living together
and everything she said about life, their life, then
being able to . . . not both of them, but him, alone,
and he wasn't even old, he wasn't even ill, he was
still the same man; just think of deciding, and getting
a gun, and going down the garden and leaving her in
bed, waiting for it, leaving her knowing what life
was going to be like afterwards, for God's sake. And
then, why did she tell us he just died, why didn't she
say? When we were talking? Because we knew all
about the rest.' She wanted to say, *I* knew, *I* understood, but went on, 'We knew, we imagined it, only
this – well, it changes everything, it means we weren't
really communicating at all!'

'I don't know what you're on about,' said Phil, and
his brown eyes were opaque, his stare blank as a cat's
startled in a roadway, shuttered with fear.

And so Lucy went away from him and wandered
down the chilly garden to stand under the apple trees
in the wet grass and wish that they could leave at
once, before it was too late, and never come back.
The heavy dew soaked her shoes and socks and

166

dragged her trousers wetly round her ankles. Here she had stood yesterday, here she stood today. Yesterday it had been the dog, tied up in the shed, waiting for Phil and Andrew and instead being taken off to the vet's. Today it was Mr Fletcher. Phil had said, 'What does it matter whether there was a dog or not?' and had dared her to believe him, to eliminate the past. What does it matter? She had told Mrs Fletcher passionately in her mind, 'No, no, I am only nineteen, you can't make me suffer these things, you can't pin it on me.' And she had been spared, spared the crux of the whole thing, spared it, that was, until too late. Lucy leaned her hot face against the spiky bark of an apple tree, her feet cold and wet in the grass around her, and for the second time that morning, wept, this time for herself, because it was too late to be told and she would never know, until she had to live it herself, what was the end and the logic of love, and what it would do to her.

'Come on, Mum, have a cup of tea or something, it'll do you good,' Andrew was saying in his soothing voice in the kitchen. 'There's no need to upset yourself like this.'

Phil sat on a stool, his long legs dangling, his face moody. Thank goodness, he was thinking, there is always Andrew to do things like this. Thank goodness that Andrew's school term has not started yet and that this Monday morning he is still here to cope. Phil thought, if I had been here on my own, I would have run out and left her, I would have disappeared. And his anger intensified at the knowledge, answering this boast from deep inside himself, that even this

was something he could not have done. The absence
of their father had hardly showed, this morning, so
smoothly had Andrew stepped into his place; and so
he, Philip, had not to face this contradiction in himself, had not to ask himself, what do I do next? He
could sit there, and be angry about Lucy and about
his mother and say to himself, over and over again,
I really can't think what all this fuss is about. He
could sit there on his stool, rigid with anger and a
sense of guilt.

'Well,' he said eventually, after watching Andrew
boil water and make tea, 'I suppose we ought to be
going. Have you got a train timetable? We're supposed to be in London tonight, to see her pa and tell
him the glad news.'

His mother turned cruelly, at once. 'Oh, Phil. Do
you have to go? Couldn't you stay another night?
Oh, it would be lovely if you could, really it would.
It would make all the difference, wouldn't it,
Andrew?'

Andrew looked sternly across at his brother, the
teapot in his hand, steam rising from the spout. He
was to Phil incongruous, so tall and thin, standing
there with a teapot and a look of parental severity.
Like a man in a flowered apron, or somebody who
does not know he has something written on his back
in chalk. 'I don't suppose it'll make much difference,'
Andrew said. 'After all, Heather and I could always
stay on an extra night, if you wanted a bit of company. We were supposed to be home by today, but I
could always get a neighbour to look in on the house
and see if everything's all right.'

'Oh, Andrew. Oh, could you? Oh, that would be

168

marvellous.' She laughed a little, uncomfortably, because what she had asked was absurd.

'Yes, well, we ought to be going,' Phil said again.
Andrew had taken the decision for him already, then.
He was dismissed. 'You'll have Andrew and Heather,
then, I think Lucy and I had better get a train this
morning.'

'Where is Lucy?' Andrew asked.

'In the garden, I think.'

'In the garden?'

'Yeah, that's what I said.'

'Bit dreary for her, it's been. Coming for a weekend
and getting tied up in all this sort of thing.'

'We're getting married,' Phil said, his anger streak-
ing to the surface. Good son and bad son, their rôles
had once again been assigned to them; after the brief
freedom of one encounter, this death, it seemed, had
made it impossible for them to meet today. There was
Andrew, with that teapot, pouring out soothing cups
of tea for everyone, and there was he, as usual about
to leave.

'It was only the shock,' Mrs Ridgley said, apologising. 'The doctor said, probably delayed shock, and I
wasn't feeling all that well, either.'

'Shock?' said Phil. 'What, keeling over like that?
It was hours after she was found. And years after he
was found,' he added as an afterthought.

'I just wasn't feeling too well,' she repeated. Why
did they stand there, accusing her, the two of them,
those boys she had brought up since they were
babies, and only through love? Why ask all these
questions, why probe her with their eyes? She was
deeply ashamed of having shown her fear in public,

before that strange man, the doctor, and her accusing sons. She faltered before them and could find no words for her defence.

'Oh, I see,' Phil said. But his tone must have been wrong, for Andrew was scowling.

'Sorry, Ma,' he said. But she felt it sweep her again, that feeling of overwhelming fear, as she sat at her own table. Everything she tried had failed. Her sons did not love her. Her husband had never really loved her. The ones you loved did not love you. She was not needed here. All these things, all these objects, her shelves of bottled fruit and tins of food, all these provisions stacked up, in case, all her clean sheets and pillowcases, all her baby clothes, put away, all her mothballs and polythene bags and piles of clothes for Oxfam, her photographs and albums and letters from the boys, her make-up box, her clothes, her scrupulous drawersful, her cupboards and boxes, all would outlast her, all be there when she was gone; she would be snuffed out, and they would throw them out and never miss her. She saw herself led as by compulsion, in a dream, out from the spruce and lighted kitchen of her ordered mind, out to leave the cleanness and the smells of baking, out through open doors where the wind howled, where blackness and emptiness could swallow her, out into the garden where winter had scraped the earth raw and the trees waved their branches, out where the fungus and mould grew and all was damp, dead, rotten; out to where the potting shed stood, its broken door creaking on a hinge, its windows cobwebbed, its roof low; to where the dog, long ago, had whined at her and scratched itself and she had drawn back in fury and

170

pity and longed to protect it, to where her sons had stood and cried, and she had longed in her heart to promise them everything, to where her husband had come and shouted at her and told her not to be a fool. And there she saw and felt the masked men who materialised out of darkness and her own fear, the hands upon her, the unwilling turning of her body, the surrender, the invasion; and she knew the gun muzzle pressed to her somewhere that would blow life out of her for ever before she could guess at what it was, and there was only one thing to cry out – 'I am sorry, I am sorry, I am sorry. . .'

'But for God's sake, Mum,' Andrew was saying. 'Sorry for what? Cheer up, there's nothing to worry about, please stop crying. Come on, have another cup of tea, and then why don't you go and lie down, you must be whacked after all this.'

'I'm sorry.' She sniffed, tried to stop her tears, pressed the handkerchief to her eyes for a moment, and then, precariously balanced, dared to take it away and look at him. Philip glanced at them both and quickly left the room.

The house seemed so quiet, and yet where could they have all gone? Phil had been talking about trains to London, but nobody had been to say goodbye. The garden was wild and blowy and empty, beating upon the glass. It was difficult to know what to do next; it must be lunchtime, nearly. There was not much point, Felicity thought, in preparing a proper meal for herself and her husband; there was the remains of that chicken and ham pie in the fridge and they could easily make do with that. 'George simply isn't

171

interested in food any more,' she heard herself tell an imaginary neighbour. 'And as for me, if I let go for a minute I run to fat. If I let go for a minute,' she addressed a crowd of listeners, and they got out their notebooks, 'if I let go for a minute . . .' But what had she been going to say? It would be so much better for them, anyway, than another huge meal. 'But the children like it,' she said confidentially, 'the children always like a good meal.' She came downstairs slowly and picked up a jersey belonging to the baby that lay in the hall and carried it to her face, feeling its softness, breathing its acrid smell. That would be something that needed doing, then, she could wash the jersey and post it after them, and perhaps put in a little letter with it, or a box of sweets. She folded it and put it away in a drawer; but then, what if they were still here? There was something in the drawer already, something flat and soft wrapped in tissue paper, her new scarf. It had lain there since Sunday breakfast-time, unnoticed. She had known it was there, she thought, but had shut it out of her mind so that she would not have to do anything about it. But now there was nobody about, now that they had all gone, she carefully drew it out. The pool of scarlet, purple and green poured from the soft white paper, it trickled through her fingers, snagging again on the rough places because it was so pure, so silk, and she so scarred with work; it lay upon the table under her gaze and she was not afraid of it. 'What a lovely present! How kind!' Joy spread across her face, excitement welled at the thought of wearing it. It would transform her, as the ball-dresses of thirty years ago could never do. She would wear it across

172

her face and glimpse the world across it with the eyes of a houri; drawing the gaze that worshipped and desired, she would twirl it around her and enter rooms upon a cloud of scarlet and purple and green, she would flash with gold like a dragonfly dipping to the water. She shut her eyes and her fingers strayed across it. To put out a hand in the darkness and feel – this! She drew it across her throat, her eyes still closed, and it was like being stroked by feathers, as if a great bird had passed. Her hand went out and snapped out the light and she stood there in the rosy dark and drew it again across her throat and rubbed it upon her cheeks, and then, for nobody would see, began hastily to unbutton her cardigan, struggle with the zip of her skirt, step out of her nylon petticoat, pull undone impatiently the fastening of her bra and the confining elastic girdle. Finally she stood there, quite naked, and drew the silk backwards and forwards, up and down her body, enfolding herself in it totally, spinning herself close with her dreams.

'Felicity!'

The light glared upon her suddenly and the look on his face was beyond all her fears, beyond criticism, beyond disapproval; he stared at her in pure horror and she clutched vaguely at the scarf to cover her but could hardly move, caught like a child peeing on the carpet, halfway through her guilty act.

'What are you doing?' he said. It was such an ordinary, such an extraordinary question, that she began to giggle, the giggles turned of their own accord to harsh sobs of laughter, tears poured down her face and she turned this way and that because there was nowhere to hide under this light away from his accusing eyes. He caught up her clothes and threw them to her, higgledy-piggledy so that she had to unhook her bra from her cardigan and sort out the tangle of her stockings; like a skin they were, all joined together, belt to stockings, petticoat to skirt.

'Put them on,' he said, and she did, slowly, turning her back on him although it did not matter any more. Suddenly it struck her, and she turned radiantly to face him, halfway through drawing on a stocking. 'I feel so much better,' she said, a smile twitching at the corners of her mouth, laughter welling up again painfully. 'It was such a lovely present!'

He did not understand. 'The scarf!' she cried, waving it at him.

'Oh, that. The one Andrew gave you.'

'Andrew? No!' she cried excitedly. 'No, I was given it to wear at the dance! So you will take me there, won't you, darling?' Her hands reached out to circle his neck, and she found it hard to understand why he, who had always wanted her to be happy, was backing away.

It was late afternoon as they approached the house, Phil driving Lucy's father's car up a road so open to the wind and sky, so flanked by space, that it seemed that the point at which they would stop could only be arbitrary. Lucy found it hard to believe that the house was actually there and that soon they would arrange with its owners for it to be bought. So much, during the last two days, had turned out to be other than it seemed, that it was hard to believe in the existence of houses. She was silent as they drove past blunt willows and the long mounds of dykes, past

174

rough roads that turned off to right and left and led to the horizon, past solitary houses where there were men feeding chickens behind wire. The afternoon was cold, the mean cold of winter already, and the sky had none of its recent brilliance but was streaked with grey and blue, blown into shapeless masses of drifting cloud that struck a wedge down to earth where the sun should be and built up towards a windy sunset.

'I'd forgotten how far it was from the village,' Phil said, breaking a long silence. He had not wanted to speak until they got there, nor risk nor move anything until he could say to her: There. There is our house. But his cold fingers on the driving-wheel and the irritation of the long and featureless road drove him to speak.

'Couldn't you shut your window?' he said. 'I'm freezing.'

'Oh, are you cold? I'm quite hot.'

'I told you, I'm freezing.'

'But the wind's nice and refreshing.'

'Oh, have it your own way,' he said. 'I'm getting used to it.' She would not answer but simply wound up the window until it was tight shut, and they sat in silence. Remarks implying bitterness, oblique attacks that hurt most through their very obliqueness, drove Lucy into terrified silence. She had not grown up hearing people say things in a tone of voice that belied the meaning. When he said, 'How extremely kind of you,' in that sharp hurtful tone, she could only turn her face and stare out of the window, count the passing willows, watch the passing road. Fear grew in her, and put out tendrils.

'Nearly there, now,' he said in a conciliatory voice, moments later, for he would never apologise.

'Yes,' said Lucy, and then, seconds later: 'Oh, Phil, look! Look at the fires!'

All at once the light grey-blue of afternoon was made the dusk of evening by a crop of little fires to right and left of them, in the wide fields that flanked the road and stretched away up a slight incline to where the house stood. Flickering, jumping, burning their patterns upon the eye, they stretched across the field of stubble, evenly ordered, like row upon row of torches at a banquet, growing a little, dying a little, each a flame that might leap from the palm of a hand and light the bearer to bed, each one smaller as it was further into the darkness than the one before, until on the summit of the slight hill, pinpricks of light only showed against the iron sky.

'Oh,' Lucy cried, 'they're like beacons, like the fires that spread news to people about the Armada! Oh, Phil, isn't it beautiful? And they go right up to our house!'

'Yes, looks like it. Though I shouldn't think our bloke has any stubble to fire. He was just doing spuds, wasn't he?' He drove on, the fires burned in endless lines, reaching up to the sky on both sides of them so that their road was a path through fire, a straight dark way to be followed between the threads of flame. The land, the solid black earth, was become a liquid sea, with waves of flame, the grey sky a bowl above them, the clouds drawing together for sunset, the sun invisible. Black against the spreading hot light of burning stubble, the willows stuck up here and there in a landscape that was otherwise as smooth

176

and wide as the ocean, its horizons somewhere lost
between sky and land.

'It's as if all the stars had fallen out of the sky and
gone on burning,' Lucy said. Her throat hurt as if
smoke from the fires had flooded it, and her eyes
pricked; the intensity of the vision was painful, the
happiness, glimpsed through glass, was also sadness,
as if one could never again be without its comple-
ment. There they were, riding along the rim of the
world, upon the edge of air and fiery darkness, yet
bound to return to the solemn grey world they had
left, in which Phil's mother sat drugged in a small
hospital room, and Mrs Fletcher was newly dead. A
flock of birds, migrating, scattered across the sky
before them, ground like black pepper against the
grey, to pass from wood to wood, calling to their kin,
collecting more and more of themselves, becoming
stronger and stronger until, blackening the whole
sky, they flew at last southwards to the sun.

'Look,' said Phil. 'Look at those birds. Amazing.
How do they know where to go?'

She looked and felt the draw of the crowd, as
though she too were small and light, an infinitesimal
spot, a grain of pepper, to be drawn upwards and
away by some force stronger than herself, something
ancient and hierarchical that would come up from
the past, from some deep collective memory of birds
and men, and take her tiny decisions from her. For
already she had decided to tell Phil on this car jour-
ney that she could not marry him; and they were
nearly there, and still she could not say it. It is not
enough, she told herself, not enough to weigh against
madness and death the knowledge of a slight body in

one's arms, a boy's head dropping in brief ecstasy on one's breast, dark eyes demanding everything and then looking easily away. I must stand on my own, she told herself. I must say that I will not marry him, and then it will all be over. She looked upwards, straining her eyes against the growing twilight, and saw the birds disappear. Phil was driving very slowly, looking around him and then turning his eyes resolutely back to the road, as if he felt that to steer a straight course was hard and necessary. I cannot become a Ridgley, Lucy told herself; there are families of rats who will tear each other to bits, ears and whiskers and all, and it is the stranger in the pack who is the first to be torn; I cannot become a rat.

'Phil,' she said, 'I suppose you know. There's something I've been thinking about. I've got to say it.'

'Here we are,' he said. 'Look, here's the house.' He turned to her, smiling his enchantment, 'Isn't it amazing, to come out here through all those fires and birds, and find it's nearly ours? Can you imagine, arriving, walking in and thinking nothing of it, because we'll have done it so often, because it'll have been ours for so long?' Beside him, she sat still and twisted her fingers round the strap of her bag in her lap. In the tree beside the house, birds seemed to be rustling. She wound down the window to breathe the cool air, and it smelt of cold chrysanthemums, but instantly she wound it up again saying, no, no, shut it out, do not hear the birds, do not even breathe the air, because it is not for you. No light showed from the house, for the farmer and his wife had already moved out, away to their new semi-detached house in the village, following their own particular

178

dream or accepting its defeat, she did not know which. It was simply a dark outline now in the growing evening, a square shape of walls and roof with trees and bushes growing like arms from its sides; the rooms inside would be all empty, with marks on the floor where the carpets and the furniture had been, bulbs hanging naked from the ceilings, electric sockets empty, all life and conversation stilled and a great silence waiting to be broken.

'Come on, then,' Phil said. He was pale this evening, fiddling in his pockets to find his cigarettes and matches with tense fingers, and his brown eyes glittered when he turned to her, to see why she was not moving to get out.

'Look, I can't,' she said with no animation; but he was not listening.

'That window in the kitchen'll still be open,' he said. 'So I'll climb in and come round to the front door to let you in.' She opened the car door obediently, and got out. It was as if all the effort, all the determination of which she was capable had been drained from her during the last few days, leaving her weak and pliable. He was ahead of her already, fumbling with the window, pushing it up, so it was no good speaking and she had none of the strength needed to shout her protest. His feet scrabbled on the gravel and disappeared into the dark hole, and she was alone outside, stuck between the car and the dark house. The noise of her own footsteps grated upon her ear, as she walked up to the front door. She heard his feet in the hall, and the bolt on the door pulled back, but there were no lights on and when she saw him it was only by a flickering match flame.

'Won't the lights go on?' She spoke almost in a whisper, so hushed and shadowed was the whole place.

'They seem to have turned the electricity off,' he said. 'But come on. It's all right.'

She hesitated still, 'Are you sure? Aren't we trespassing?' When one was afraid, there seemed suddenly to be all sorts of laws that could be broken. But it was impossible now to say once again, 'I can't.'

'What an extraordinary thing for you to say!' Phil laughed, and she wanted to tell him, 'Sssh, be quiet!' 'Come on, darling, stop fussing, we can see our way with matches all right. What are you afraid of?'

Was it that this boy, her friend and lover, was all at once older, a man opening the door of his house and forcing her to come in?

'Nothing, really,' she said, and stepped across the threshold; he took her arm to steady her in the reeling darkness around the tiny flame. The match went out, in his fingers, and he dropped it and let go of her again to strike another. The fragile light moved again over the unknown features of his face and his seriousness as he concentrated on keeping it alight, holding the head of the match downwards. He began to walk slowly up the hill ahead of her, and she followed. The house smelt of damp and cold already, as if nobody had lived there. Her fingers trailed over the bumpy surface of the patterned wallpaper, flowers and squirls embossed. She was all at once afraid to speak to him, for there seemed to be nothing worth saying. At the foot of the stairs she stumbled over a loose floorboard but caught at the banister to save herself, and he did not turn. They mounted the stairs, his match a ghost flare upon walls and patterns and uncurtained windows, and on the landing he paused to light another, intent on what he was doing. 'Well,' he said, as they stood at the top and the doors of the bedrooms stood wide around them. 'Here we are.'

'Yes,' she said. He lit a cigarette and the small red point was the first comfortable, ordinary thing. 'Can I have one, please?' she asked him. They smoked together, leaning against the banister rail, the window behind them a sea of clouds and pale light, as the moon came out and sailed between the banks of darkness. Lucy puffed hard at her cigarette and dropped ash on the floor with constant little flicks of her fingers, and could find nothing to say. Phil dropped his cigarette with a long butt unsmoked, and trod it underfoot. 'Won't it mark the floor?' she said, without thinking.

'Does it matter?' he said.

'Well, doesn't it?'

'Oh, Lucy,' he said, and took her in his arms, holding her so hard that she could scarcely breathe; her face was flattened against his rough jersey, her nose bent against his breast-bone, her knees pressed back so that if he had let go she would have fallen. He began to steer her backwards through one of the open doors, and she was too limp, too weak to struggle for breath or freedom, but followed his pressure like a dancing partner toppling over in some fierce tango, her feet hardly touching the ground. He brought her down to the ground and began kissing her all over her face and neck, while she moved her head from side to side and tried to speak, but was prevented again and again by the interruption of his mouth, so

that only little grunts and mumbles could escape her;
he pushed her down, so that she lay on the boards
and was all shoulder-blades and hip bones, ground in
pain under his weight, for he covered her completely
and hurt her with his surprising heaviness; as if she
had been thrown to the floor of a warehouse and
covered with sacks of sand, she was helpless. He was
pulling at her clothes and this time she could do
nothing to help or hinder him, for her hands lay
somewhere miles away, pinned to the floor; she simply
felt him tug at her shirt until it was open down the
front and pull at her bra so that his hands could go
in and cover her breasts; and the safety-pin that had
held it together since yesterday came open and stuck
into her back so that she cried out and squirmed to
get away from it, and her nipples felt sandpapered
by his rough wool until he saw that he was hurting
her and sat up for a minute to pull both jersey and
shirt off over his head in one movement and move her
to lie upon the softness of his clothes. She lay there
and watched him undo his belt and unzip his trousers,
looked down at her own body, the hillocks of her
breasts sloping away from her, the small round hole
of the navel, the crumpled trousers half pulled away,
and thought, I had not thought of this. I had not
planned anything like this. And this is my body, this
is me, and here he is behaving as if I belonged to him.
She was like putty, like dough to him, as he pushed
her about and she felt nothing but the unkindness of
his hands and mouth, and she lay under him, retreating to the floorboards, sulky with fear. But he looked
down at her and saw her face, and smiled more
gently, ran a hand slowly and with infinite care over

182

the contours of one side and slipped down to lay his dark head upon her thighs and pursue her with the incredible kindness of his tongue while she lay looking down at the black bush that lay heavy on her; his face hidden, as in sudden humility, his white legs stretched across the floor. Her hands reached his shoulders and moved across smooth and slippery flesh. And simultaneously they drew each other close and began to rock with the profundity of the new feeling that reared like a wave over them and left them gasping, incredulous, like drowning humans who see in the watery depths, before water rushes into eyes, lungs and bowels, the whole of their lives spread out. Ages passed, and they lay swamped, exhausted, hot and cold shivering through them, the hard floor and the cold night air of the room pressing them together to cling to their last warmth, the rivers of love drying cold upon their bodies until Phil flung out an arm and reached for his scattered clothes to cover them both. Lucy curled close to him, teeth chattering, under the scant cover of jerseys and trousers and underclothes, and tried to find words to tell him, but was still dumb. Trust, she wanted to say, trust and love and certainty. There were words that said it all, words that she had never before understood but had heard others use, in some perversion of language. Grace and understanding and healing. But her mouth was shattered with the tremblings of shock, her lips were cold and her teeth would not be quiet. He covered her so that all the cold must be received upon his own body, and wrapped his whole length round her, and said, 'Lucy, Lucy,' till her own name rang in her ears, another new word, another revelation. 'Lucy, Lucy,' he said, as if she had just been discovered. The window rattled with a rising breeze from the night, and something pattered and scuffled in a corner – a mouse, perhaps, a bird in the eaves – and eventually they got up together, with difficulty, and sorted out their clothes. Lucy's hands shook, and he helped her to dress herself, after they had hunted, laughing, for the necessary safety-pin. As they left the room, feet unsteady and her body stiff from the floor, he said, 'This can be our bedroom.' Marriage, she thought, marriage and a house, those are words too, and they mean other things to other people, they are lying words, simplifications. This can be our bedroom. The old house, like a shell, like a home for a hermit crab, stood darkened behind them, letting them go as easily as it had let them in. The room was theirs, but there were others, hotel rooms, rooms in houses, squares of earth under an open sky, cabins in ships and berths in trains, other homes that awaited them. They got into the car without speaking, and before Phil started the engine, he leaned and enfolded her again, and brought her on his lips some of the familiarity, the taste of passion, warm and good to eat. The cough of the car's engine as it turned over was alarmingly loud, they had been so quiet. He drove it in a three-point turn and started down the drive; and on the edge of the road, he paused, to let her look, she thought, to let her remember. The fires glowed still in the darkness, but were nearly out, as if the encroaching coldness of the October night had shuttered them. The land sloped away before them easily, and then was flat to the horizon. The moon moved out from behind a cloud and hung in clear space, whitening the land. Lucy sighed, and touched his hand on the gearstick, grateful for the moment, the first pause.

Phil said, 'That's how it'll be.'

And she said, 'Yes.'

For everything else was for others, who did not know. The small daily death of boredom, the threat that crept out and was madness, the incongruity of death.

Phil said, 'Everybody thinks they'll be different, I suppose.' And she said, 'Yes, but we know.' Doubt, rationality, prudence; the accumulated posessions of twenty years of life, weapons that had lain low and vigilant under her passions, her waywardness, were finally locked away. They had been painful to acquire, but she saw them go with scarcely a backward look, for it was too late. She had embarked, as she saw it, on something which could not be denied or changed. Decision had been outworn. She had decided not to marry him, but it was too late. He was flowing in and around her, he had re-created her and made her somehow his, and if marriage was what he wanted, marriage was what she wanted too. Her will, like the fires on the stubble fields in the October evening, was damped and dying; she was weak and tired and cold and amazed with passion and, at last, she needed him. To have escaped now this woman's fate, this need, this dire channel of love that led who knows where, to have marched on, red hair flying and chin tipped with independence, searching singly for the truth, she would have had to be somebody else. This she thought, as Phil drove on and the fields and fens flew past them, and the willows, drawn in charcoal on the sky, and the deep dykes and the plotted rows of celery and turnip, and the earth like chocolate that she would get to know so well, the earth from which she would grow; yesterday, she thought, I was a person, and today I am another person; and who knows what I may be tomorrow?

It did not seem long afterwards that Mrs Fletcher's house was sold. The Ridgleys had not often turned to look at it, as they walked down their drive or came back up the road from a brisk leg-stretch before tea; for it seemed closed up, after Mrs Fletcher's death, and there was something embarrassing about its tight-shut windows and its finally locked door; it was stripped of every covering by the colder wind of winter; even the virginia creeper hung in brown, dead wisps and could not hide it, the trees in the garden grew away from it and stuck their bare branches straight up in the air. The garden had that sodden thick look of abandoned winter gardens, the potting shed roof caved in and the paths were blocked with wads of dead leaves. She had always pottered about in her garden when she was alive, even in the most bitter weather, straightening things and tying them back, freeing her delicate plants from the weight of leaves or snow, shaking their twigs for them, so that they might have a chance to start again. She used to bend slowly and straighten slowly, one hand to her back. She used to carry a heavy wooden basket down the garden, and wear ankle socks over her stockings, and cracked leather gloves. Phil at least remembered her like that. She had had an old hat, that could have belonged to a man, and sometimes she would tilt it back on her head and peer at the sky, sometimes take it off to pat her untidy bun of hair, and replace it so that no stray wisps could fall across her brow.

Mrs Ridgley, Felicity (though little had come her way), was back after two months from her stay in the hospital, her eyes cloudier perhaps, movements slower and more deliberate than they had been before. She had come home in time for the wedding, and had worn daffodil yellow to the register office, clasping her hands together as the brief ceremony happened, with silence and amazement. George had allowed her only a little champagne. The world had seemed all at once very well-organised. She kissed Lucy on the cheek, twice, and waved a gloved hand as the car drove away. But now she was at the bathroom window, a cloth in her hand to polish the taps, and in the matted grass of Mrs Fletcher's lawn, next door, a small black and white cat sat and washed itself. It got up, stretched, and began to pounce on things that might have moved under the grass; but the grass and the leaves were too sodden, too heavy to play, and the cat sat down as if it hoped that nobody had been watching. Felicity wetted the cloth and carefully wiped the glass of the window, the smeared, spotted and breathed-on glass of bathroom windows behind which people have been shaving, examining their teeth and squeezing spots. There – it was clear again. She could see the thin trees in Mrs Fletcher's garden; only a few more doddering leaves to go, and it would be proper winter, long, bleak, irrevocable. Days of iron earth and leaden sky. Nights from which one woke aching with the desire for sleep. Hours of wiping floors after muddy shoes, hours made pointless by pointless care. She sighed, and put the top on the toothpaste tube, but then remembered what they had told her at the hospital. She did not have to do that any more; there was a woman coming in to clean in the mornings, and George would bring up her breakfast in bed, and a visitor from the hospital would call once a week, all solicitude. The winter would go on just the same, meanly, but outside the locked doors of her house. This year, it would not be allowed to intrude. She was relieved, but puzzled; what then would she do? There was not even any need to polish the taps and put the top on the toothpaste tube, let alone clean floors and make beds and turn out the kitchen cup-boards. They said she was doing too much, at the hospital. But what else was there to do? She looked down at her hands, which were still whiter and softer from her idleness than they had ever been since George took them first in his. What was one to do with hands like that? Downstairs in the hall there were library books and flowers that had been sent; and bowls of fruit, as if she were really ill, and maga-zines, and knitting. She had entered her kitchen first as a stranger, coming back from the hospital, and had noticed all the scratches and dust that had happened as if she did not exist. 'There'll be nothing for you to worry about here,' they said, 'Mrs Phillips'll come in and do the lunch, and leave you something for yours and your husband's supper. And she's to do all the washing up in the morning.' So she had not dared to disobey, not even dared to let the thought cross her mind, but had closed the kitchen door as if that were somebody else's domain, and gone to sit quietly in the living-room, to listen to Woman's Hour and knit a little coat for Jonathan and breathe with each deep and panicking breath the sour smell of the chrysanthemums. That was two days ago, and they had still not told her what she was supposed to do. She put down her cloth as if afraid that she might be surprised at her illegal work, and then saw that there was a couple standing outside Mrs Fletcher's house, looking up at the big orange and white sign that said For Sale. She stared. Surely people like that could not be thinking of buying it? Like that? She meant, normal, ordinary; deserving. The sight of them made her catch her breath, think swiftly, Oh, no. Impossible. They would never buy that house and settle next door. The soaked and gap-toothed fence, the bleak black sticks in the garden, that shuttered emptiness, surely they saw all this, surely they knew it was hopeless? They had come in a car, and it was parked a little way down the road, as if they had driven almost past the house without stopping before realising that *that* was the one. She opened the window, hoping to catch a little of what they said across the raw distance. Somebody ought to tell them. But tell them what? That there had been a suicide in the garden shed? That an old woman had died of a heart attack with her fingers caught under a broken sash? That a woman lived next door whose twenty years of residence and marriage in her house had led her, gibbering, to the asylum? People died everywhere; people had nervous breakdowns; people rotted, perplexed in their separate houses, shut in by walls and windows, from here to John O'Groats. But what else could one say? Simply that next door to the Ridgleys was no place for a young couple to live? She did not know, she felt confused by her urge to tell them something, to call out across the garden and the drive and give them some kind of warning, and was afraid too these days of her own promptings. But soon it would be too late, for they would have opened the door and gone inside. They were young, quite smart, and probably childless. Married, oh, yes. There was an impatience in the man's movements, an anxiety in the woman's, that she recognised. He was gesturing on the doorstep, impatient to go in, yet he would not take the step without her; she was perhaps aware that in there, in those empty rooms, a life awaited her which would engulf her but offer her nothing in return but the cold touch of objects, soon to be dust. She was perhaps thinking, if I don't go in, I shall have more of a chance. She seemed to be examining a flowerbed, not as if it interested her, but as if it would look too stupid to stare at nothing, and as if to look stupid were in itself a crime. Felicity stared at the husband, examining him for signs of tenderness, and finding none. He was obviously a clever man. He was also tall, tidily dressed, pink-and-white skinned, with crisp curly hair. He had a large nose, which saved his face from looking too bland and babyish, and large, well-shaped white hands, with which he urged his wife to hurry up, and stop daydreaming, and come and look inside. He looked at his watch; evidently he was late for another appointment. Felicity felt relieved for Phil and Lucy, that when they came back from their honeymoon it would be to a flat in London, for the moment; there would be none of these decisions. The girl, clutching a little bundle of gloves, scarf and handbag in front of her, crossed the gravel drive to obey him. She wore a fashionable beige trouser suit with a long jacket, smooth, well-cut, 'uncluttered' as they said: but the bag, the scarf, the gloves, the hair and the anxious little face were all clutter, clutter collected, thought Felicity Ridgley in her brand-new clarity, in defence. But she was cold, she felt dispirited and all at once even unwilling to help. She closed the window and saw the couple instinctively look up together, their faces defenceless in their surprise as they saw, no doubt, her face against the glass. She groped for a convention, ashamed that they had seen her spy on them; she longed to tell them that she sympathised, that she was on their side. The man took no notice, but covered his face again with the mask he had worn; the woman shyly raised her hand in greeting in return. They turned their backs on her, and went into the house.